HER BILLIONAIRE RANCHER BOSS

GENEVIEVE TURNER

Chapter 1

PILAR LOPEZ TUCKED THE ENVELOPE BEHIND her tablet computer, shifting the corners this way and that. And never completely concealing it.

Could he see it? That was all that mattered.

He being her boss, Benedict Merrill. Sitting behind his desk in a bright white button-down shirt, long legs stretched out before him in starched and pressed Wranglers. She couldn't see from here, but she imagined his battered black ropers were crossed at the ankle.

When a man ran one of the largest cattle-ranches-turned-hotel-and-resort in Southern California—not to mention the stock horse operation—he could wear Western business casual to work. Not that Benedict was casual. He was tough, efficient, almost cold.

Too bad his demeanor didn't chill her attraction to him.

Only three more months. As soon as you give him that letter.

But not now. He was frowning—not at her, but at some expense report. Not a good time then.

She'd only been telling herself that for a week.

Today. She would definitely do it today. Just not at this particular moment.

"Tell Liliana," he said in his deep voice, "that the feed bill for her horses was too damn high this month. I don't know what she's feeding them, but it sure ain't alfalfa based on the price I saw. She needs to get a better price if she's gonna buy that much."

"I can do that." She made a note on her tablet to talk to Benedict's younger sister. Liliana ran the stock operations, although Benedict kept a close eye on everything. He treated his siblings with the same businesslike reserve he treated his employees. At least on company time. She guessed he was more approachable off the clock, considering that his siblings seemed to like him.

There was nothing in his office to hint at some hidden warmth though. Spartan was a good word for it—in the lacking things sense, not the naked warrior sense. He liked everything squared away and in its proper place. Very type A, Mr. Benedict Merrill.

The sparsity of his office décor wasn't meant to highlight the man himself, but that's exactly what it did. You couldn't look anywhere but at him.

At least Pilar couldn't.

He reached across the desk, the light catching the heavy watch he wore, his sleeves rolled up to reveal sinewy forearms, rough with hair and golden skinned. Her stomach clenched as she fought her reaction.

The first four years she'd worked for him, she'd been as crisp, as unfeeling, as he was. On the inside and on the outside. But the past year... she'd begun to notice him. Like *notice* him.

He tapped a finger on the paper in his hand. "Luke wants to meet about this?"

Luke ran the resort. Liliana and Luke and Benedict, another generation of Merrills to run things in Cabrillo.

And Josh, but no one spoke of Josh. At least not to Benedict's face.

"Would you like me to set it up?" She looked down at the tablet, fingers poised over the small keyboard, waiting for him to tell her yes.

He didn't.

She glanced up to find him watching her. His gaze pressed on her with a weight it had never had before, her bones seeming to shift under it.

She dropped her eyes back to the tablet, resisting the urge to rub the goose bumps from her arms.

Be cool. Of course he's looking at you—what else is there to look at?

"Pilar?"

A tiny shiver danced down her spine at the way he said her name—a softly breathed *P* to open it and ending on a rolling *R*. Just as it was meant to be pronounced.

He leaned toward her, a hank of dark brown hair falling across his brow, his blue eyes narrowing. "Is everything all right?"

She shifted in the chair, her skirt dragging up her thighs half an inch. Damn. She didn't want to have to tug down her skirt in front of him. She froze, hoping to arrest its climb. "Everything's fine. When should I schedule the meeting?"

He leaned even closer and put on a reassuring—and devastating—smile. "If there's anything the matter, you can tell me. We're friends, you know."

Friends. Friends shared jokes and secrets and mundanities. A friend didn't take dictation for another friend.

But that wasn't quite fair. They might not be friends, but

he did care. She wouldn't have this job if he didn't. His solicitude made her attraction to him that much more painful.

She pulled up her *I'm a friendly and competent admin* smile, the one she used on everyone who came through his office. "Everything's great."

The envelope beneath her tablet poked through the knit of her tights to scrape the skin of her knee, a potent reminder that she was a liar.

He sat back, hooked his thumbs into his belt, his hands framing the buckle he'd won for team roping in high school. His picture in the paper for that had showcased a wide smile on his younger, easier face. He was in the paper these days too, but for things like opening a new Boys & Girls Club and donating to the food pantry; he took his responsibilities to the area seriously.

"All right then," he said, back to steady neutrality. "Tell Luke we'll meet tomorrow afternoon."

"Will do. And the preliminary agreement for Mr. Farrell? Did you want to work on that now?"

He ran a hand through his hair, pushing it back into place. Which was a shame, since he'd looked so delectable before.

No. It was good that he was less attractive this way. Very good.

"Let's stop for lunch and pick up again after."

She nodded in response and gathered up her tablet— and that stupid letter she was too much of a coward to give him. She headed for the door, her kitten heels click-click-clicking along the tile floor. She shut his office door quietly behind her, then went to sit at her own desk, scooting herself into place. Kitten heels were cute for bounding through the halls, but the slick soles made her feel as if she were scrabbling whenever she moved her chair.

Her own workspace was a little more welcoming than Benedict's. No windows—her view was of the ranch logo, the words "Honoring the past, looking toward the future," emblazoned below it. Two desks—one for her and a spare— a couple of peace lilies that were overflowing their planters, some orchids for color, and a bromeliad just because. She sometimes wondered what people thought, going from the indoor forest she'd created here to the austerity of Benedict's office.

She checked the moisture level of the bark in the orchid on her desk and sighed. Lunchtime. She could head outside to eat her lunch, but the red button on the e-mail program flashing 52 at her put that idea to rest. She had to work through some of those e-mails. Lunch at her desk it was.

She pulled open a drawer, slipped the letter under her purse where it couldn't taunt her, then slammed the drawer shut when Benedict came out of the office.

He stopped, stared at her. "Everything okay?"

She folded her hands in an imitation of innocence. "Great," she chirped. "See you in about an hour."

He stayed right where he was... and *cocked* his eyebrow. Just the one, coming up in a dead-sexy lift.

Had he ever done that before? It looked like he was about to call her a naughty girl and spank her.

Get a grip, Pilar. He only thinks you're acting weird. Which you totally are.

Thank God she was leaving in three months, because her libido was taking over her subconscious at this point. Give it enough time in Benedict Merrill's presence and it'd take over her conscious brain as well.

She kept her hands folded, her smile tight on her face, and prayed she looked professional and not deranged.

That brow of his slowly returned to its normal spot, and

he turned to leave, giving her a fine view of his ass in those Wranglers. A fine and torturous view.

She shook her head and smashed her fist into her forehead for good measure. *Idiot.* She meant herself, but a bit of that irritation was directed at him. Why did he have to pull that stunt with his eyebrow? And coming out right when he had, just as she was hiding the letter and scaring her half to death? That had been a close call.

Of course, after lunch she'd hand over the letter and there'd be nothing more to hide. Sighing, she pulled out her peanut butter sandwich. Hurriedly downing her sandwich with her left hand while pecking out replies with her right, she tilted one ear toward the hallway in case someone came. An admin should never be caught with a palm full of sticky peanut butter.

Once the unanswered e-mails were down to sixteen and her sandwich was entirely gone, she click-clacked down the hall to the washroom. These offices—and the entire resort —looked like those a mission might have, with red tile floors and white adobe walls. If a mission had been devoted to luxurious relaxation and not religious conversion.

The surroundings made her feel very much like an admin in a movie, with her skirt that highlighted and smoothed her curves—a hard thing to find in her size—and a shirt that showed just enough cleavage to say *Hello* rather than *Look at me!* At least, if they made movies about overweight Mexican girls instead of Jennifer Lopez. Who wasn't overweight. Or Mexican.

The bathroom was tiled in vibrant shades of blue and yellow, a sultan's hamam by way of California. She washed her hands, the peanut butter smell faintly lingering under the floral soap, brushed her teeth, and went rooting in her bag for her lip stain. She made a kissy face in the mirror with her newly bright lips. Please God, let the makeup company never discontinue this color—it was hard to find a red that looked good on her and was appropriate for work. Maybe she should stockpile it—how long did lip stain last? Like, cockroach long? Or maybe just government-cheese long?

She click-click-clicked her way back to the desk to deal with those last sixteen e-mails. Her hands were poised above the keyboard as she tried to think of the best way to word this refusal, when Benedict came back.

He strode toward his office door, not in a rush but clearly not wishing to waste time. He went past her desk... and stopped. And smiled at her.

An answering smile began to spread across her face, hot and quick as a pool of gasoline catching a spark.

Then it guttered and died.

The letter.

No more putting it off.

"Ready?" he asked.

She nodded dumbly, and he disappeared into his office.

Coming to stand before him, the envelope clutched between her fingers, she felt as shaky and sick as when... well, as when she'd been standing before him five years ago with another piece of paper in her hands. Her résumé that time, instead of a letter of resignation.

She'd been there ostensibly to apply for the admin job, but they both knew why she was truly there: to ask for yet another Merrill handout.

And because Benedict was kind and considerate, he'd given her the job. She'd worked as hard as she could, aiming to be the ideal secretary, but no matter how well she performed, it couldn't erase the fact that she never would have been considered if her parents hadn't died. If she hadn't suddenly found herself responsible for her thirteen-year-old brother.

Benedict's initial impulse of charity had meant that she could keep Javier and herself fed and housed. And could amass a sizable college fund for her brother. She was grateful—but she also wanted to be free of Merrill charity.

Which was why she waited before him now, clutching her letter of resignation. And she'd give it to him just as soon as she found her voice.

He set his knuckles on the desk and rose from his chair as she stood there in silence. "Now I know something is wrong." His voice vibrated with worry—actually *vibrated*—setting off tiny tremors in her limbs. "Please tell me. I want to help."

She nearly whimpered. There had been nothing like that from him when she'd first applied. It had been all impersonal efficiency layered over what was really happening: "*Yes, you're the best qualified person, I'm happy to hire you,*" instead of "*You need my help.*"

She closed her eyes, reached for indifference.

People leave jobs all the time. You're not ungrateful or resentful. You're allowed to move on.

She almost believed it.

Eyes wide, shoulders back, heels snapping, she marched to him, the envelope hanging at the end of her stiffly outstretched arm. He snatched it from her before she could say anything.

"What's this?" he rumbled as he tore into it.

"It's, um..." God, she still couldn't say it. And he was already reading it!

His gaze snapped back and forth as he scanned it. "What the fuck?" he snarled before throwing it to his desk.

Whoa. He never swore like that. Ever. She blinked at the letter lying there between them.

He pointed at her. "Sit down."

The force of her butt hitting the seat snapped her out of her odd mood. This—his reaction—was all wrong. People left jobs—even people who worked for him. He'd need a few months to adjust to a new admin, but snapping at her? *Swearing?*

"Yeah, that's my resignation letter," she said. "Which you already know."

Snark. Her favorite weapon in awkward situations. Sometimes he even laughed at her little asides.

He wasn't laughing now. He sat down himself, pinning her with a look that was intense. Almost mad.

No, not mad. She'd seen him irritated, and this was different. Hotter. And sadder, all at the same time.

"I won't let you leave," he said starkly.

The room seemed to rise, spin three hundred sixty degrees with her as the unmoving center, then settled back into place, everything as it was. Only not quite. Things gleamed a little brighter, edges were a little harder, shadows a little murkier. And Benedict, a house cat turned into a mountain lion, his sharp teeth lengthened into fangs.

Stop it. That was crazy. He was only pissed that he'd have to train a new assistant.

"I'm pretty sure you have to let me leave," she pointed out. "The Thirteenth Amendment and all that."

He blinked at her. "Did you just invoke the Thirteenth Amendment?"

"Yeah," she admitted. "I guess I did."

He reached for the letter again, his fingers pinching and releasing the folds but never opening it. "Of course you can leave." His voice took on a funereal hush. "I... I can't make you stay."

She frowned at the letter herself, at his fingers plucking purposelessly at it. It sounded almost as if he *wanted* to make her stay. But there wasn't anything deeper in his protests. Her own frustrated attraction was adding nuances that simply weren't there.

"Why do you want to leave?" he asked. "Pilar"—his voice went to a register of pleading she'd never heard before from him—"God, I thought you were happy here. With me."

Was this a discussion about her resignation or a breakup? Things were getting very weird. "Of course I'm happy to work for you."

His frown deepened. What the hell? She'd just said she was happy to work for him. She'd thought he'd be pissed and that he'd try his best to hide it. That reaction she'd been prepared to deal with.

But this... *guilt trip?* It wasn't fair. She'd been an excellent secretary for five years. She'd *raised her brother* for five years. She deserved to snatch something for herself, and she wasn't going to feel guilty about it. Or at least she wasn't going to let that ball of guilt forming in her gut stop her plans.

"So why?" he demanded.

"Javier graduates in three months," she began.

"I know," he said shortly. As if he had it marked on a calendar or something.

"After that, it's time for something different." Somewhere far away from Cabrillo. And from Benedict Merrill.

But not too far. She still had to keep an eye on Javier.

Benedict slid his knuckles along the edge of the desk, the menace in the gesture made ice crust her spine. Man, he was freaking out here. And freaking her out.

"What different thing do you want to do in Cabrillo?"

If he was going to offer her another job… But of course he would, if he assumed she was staying. The Merrills had a finger in every pie in this town. Hell, they *owned* half the town.

Which was part of why she wanted to escape.

"I'm planning on moving. Maybe to LA. Maybe even farther," she said defiantly. She appreciated the opportunity he'd given her, but now she was going to go make some opportunities of her own, in a place not *his* own.

"You really are leaving," he said slowly, his brows drawing together.

Finally. Some of this was getting through to him.

"Yep," she said. "But in three months. Plenty of time to find a replacement and help train them."

"Really?" He cocked that eyebrow again, disbelief dripping from the word.

How come he'd never done that eyebrow thing before? Although it was probably for the best since it made her imagine naughty things. Even while in this weird situation where she was trying to resign and he was being stubborn about it.

"I would never leave you high and dry like that."

"Wouldn't you?" A dark purr. A darkly sexy purr.

She gripped the arms of her chair, the edges sinking into the soft bits of her palms, and ordered her blood to slow.

A purr? What was wrong with her? He wasn't trying to be sexy—he was annoyed. A man as controlled as he was, he liked things to stay the same. Training a new admin, no matter how competent, was going to put his mood into a kink.

Kink. Kinky.

She was heading into sexual harassment territory here. *Focus.*

"No, I wouldn't." She sat straighter, put on a blank expression. At least one of them could be rational about this. "I'm giving you three months' notice—more than enough time to find a suitable admin."

He leaned back in his chair, but his stance was anything but easy. He hooked his thumbs in his belt, and she ordered her stupid libido to ignore that. "What if I think you're irreplaceable?"

She busted out a laugh before she could catch herself, then faked a cough to try to cover it. "Uh, no. I'm not. After a while, you won't even know I'm gone."

"Won't I?"

She had to believe he meant something else with all this, that he wasn't really trying to... well, trying to seduce her. Because that would make leaving all the more painful.

"You won't," she insisted. "We'll find someone great. They'll shadow me for a while—the transition will be entirely seamless." For the both of them.

"Mmm." He took his lower lip between his thumb and forefinger, tugged a bit.

Now see, why did he have to do something like that? Something that made her think about kissing him?

Make this easy. Just accept my resignation and thank me for my time here.

He released his lip. "You know what? I can't discuss this with you right now."

"Oh." She half rose, then sat right back down. "Wait. No. Why can't you just accept my resignation? What's going on here?"

She needed him to be as he usually was—calm, cold, professional—and he simply refused. If some snappishness got him to sit down and behave, she'd be as nippy as a terrier.

"Nothing nefarious," he drawled. He pulled his jacket from the back of his chair and shrugged into it.

Where was he going? He had nothing on his calendar. She should know—she scheduled it for him.

"You can't be leaving." Her voice climbed toward shrillness but didn't quite reach it.

He did that stupid eyebrow thing again. "I can. I am. We'll discuss this over dinner. Seven, in the bar."

He was ordering her. He'd never ordered before. He'd always asked. And used *please* and *thank you*, no doubt like his mama taught him. She wanted to say something very, very foul in Spanish, but she didn't dare. He spoke it almost as well as she did.

He went for the door, stiff legged and tight jawed.

Something else was going on. Because her resignation should not have caused this. Maybe something had happened to Josh? But Benedict had been in a fine mood before...

Javier.

"But what about Javier?" she called after him. Someone had to feed her little brother. "What will he do for dinner if I'm eating here?"

He paused in the doorway, his expression thunderous. "He's eighteen and he can't feed himself?"

"He..." She didn't want to admit that some nights Javier didn't come home, that she didn't know where he went. That she sat up and waited in the kitchen, wondering if she was going to get a call from the police. Or the morgue. "I guess he'll be okay."

Lately she suspected that he wouldn't be okay at all, but she wasn't admitting that to Benedict.

"Seven," he ordered again, hand on the doorknob.

He was really going to leave in the middle of a workday? They hadn't even started on the afternoon to-do list.

"Wait," she began, "didn't you want to do the preliminary—"

He shut the door behind him.

"I guess not," she called in farewell. "And you shut me in."

She turned to gather her things, catching sight of her letter on the desk, gaping half open, the words hidden. He hadn't technically accepted her resignation. Which left her where?

"Well, shit," she muttered.

Chapter 2

PILAR CALLED UP THE HOME screen on her phone once more—6:58 p.m. She opened her text messages, the last one she sent popping up.

Eating at work. Want me to bring you something? Text me when you get home.

No response from Javier, although she'd sent it two hours ago.

But that was usual, this electronic silence of his. Along with his very real silences when they were face-to-face. She already knew what he'd say if she confronted him: that his phone was dead, that he'd turned it off to study, that he'd run out of text messages for the month.

She hoped that last wasn't the case. The last time he'd run out of texts, the overage charges on the bill had almost made her pass out.

Better that than him being sick though. Or in jail. Or dead.

She tossed her phone back into her bag, hooking her leg more firmly around the barstool to keep from sliding off. The kitten heels she'd been so enamored with earlier were pinching her feet, and she couldn't wait to get this skirt off and into some yoga pants. And slip out of her bra. That was going to be heaven.

But first, dinner with Benedict. They'd had dinner together before, but only when they'd been working late together on something.

Of course, she hadn't tried to resign before.

"Pilar!"

Liliana came bounding past the immense walnut horse-shoe bar, chestnut hair flying, her long legs eating up the distance as her boot heels drummed out a staccato beat.

"Liliana." She smiled wide in greeting. It was impossible to be sad when Liliana smiled at her. "How are you?"

"Great, now that I'm off the clock." She turned to the bartender. "Just a root beer please."

Pilar didn't think she'd ever seen any of the Merrill siblings drink alcohol. She was sure they did—Liliana'd had too much fun at the NFRs just last month not to have been drinking—but they never did it on the resort grounds. Of course, with the whole Josh incident—which had happened right before Pilar had taken the job—their attitude made sense.

"Are you off the clock too?"

"I guess?" Pilar spread her palms in an approximation of the size of her confusion. "Benedict wanted to meet for dinner."

"Ooooh." Liliana made it sound like Benedict had asked to meet for sex.

"It's not like that. We're meeting to discuss my resignation."

"What?" Liliana's screech punched at Pilar's eardrums. And probably the eardrums of everyone in a five-mile radius.

"Javier's going to be graduating soon, and I just..." She shrugged, the stiffness in her shoulders making the motion jerky. "It's time for a change."

"You're going to tell Benedict that tonight?" Liliana was tentative, as if stepping out on a tightrope.

"I already told him earlier today."

Liliana slammed her glass onto the bar, condensation flying from it. "What did he say?"

"He was upset. Naturally." And totally weird about the whole thing, but they'd work all that out tonight over dinner.

"Naturally," the other woman echoed rather sarcastically.

"You know how he is." Defensiveness crept into her voice. Benedict had a right to be upset that his admin was leaving. "He likes things to stay the same."

"Yeah." Pronounced as if Liliana knew something she didn't. "What are you going to do instead?"

"Move somewhere new. Maybe LA, maybe San Luis Obispo—it's so pretty there—"

"And cold." Liliana gave an exaggerated shudder.

Pilar laughed. "It's only a four-hour drive from here, not the Great White North."

Liliana shared her laughter for a moment, then her expression faded into uncertainty. "How, uh, how is Javier doing? On track to graduate?"

No. "Yes. I was hoping he'd apply to a CSU, but he wants to go to the junior college here first. Get his feet wet, you know?"

Wow, she'd actually said all that with a straight face. She'd saved enough for him to go to a CSU if he wanted, but as far as she could tell the only place Javier wanted to go was to his friend Ernesto's house and the pool hall. And to sleep.

When he did bother to come home, he promptly went to his room and shut the door.

She was failing him, but she had no idea how to un-fail him. And she wasn't admitting any of that to Liliana. Or Liliana's older brother.

"That's good," Liliana was saying. "It's been what, five years since your parents..." She went pink and cleared her throat.

Funny how reluctant people were to admit that Pilar's parents had died. As if she herself hadn't realized it and they were afraid to tell her.

"Since, uh, you had to take over," Liliana finished. "You deserve some fun."

Yeah, it was going to be great fun, worrying about whatever stupid, dangerous thing Javier might be doing but having no legal way to stop him. It sure was a hell of a lot fun now.

"Pilar."

She almost slid off the seat at Benedict's voice in her ear. Did he have to make her name sound so sexy? Her school nickname of "Pilaf" had proved that her name wasn't the least bit sexy. So why were her nipples tightening, dragging torturously along the lace of the bra she couldn't wait to take off?

"Yes?" Her kitten heels hit the floor with an ungraceful clunk, and she winced as the pain in her feet came roaring back.

"Are you all right?" He slid his hand around to cup her elbow, and her pulse shot up to eleven.

Stop it stop it stop it...

"Great," she squeaked.

"Hey, big bro." Liliana's smirk was smug enough to choke on. "Having dinner with Pilar, huh?"

"I love you too," he answered. "Now get lost."

That was rather impolite. "Would you like to join us?" Pilar asked to apologize for Benedict's rudeness.

"No, she wouldn't," Benedict growled. The hand on her elbow tightened and pulled her closer to him. "Follow me."

Liliana gave them a little waggle of her fingers—and a shit-eating grin—in farewell.

Benedict guided her—really, it was that graceful, no dragging—into one of the private dining rooms in the steakhouse. There was white linen and china and candles and a bottle of champagne chilling by the side of the table.

Holy shit. First he said he couldn't accept her resignation, and then he pulled this.

"The bar would have been fine."

He held out her chair. "No, it wouldn't have. Not for this."

Oooh. That sounded foreboding, and ominous... and kind of sexy.

He kept his hand on her elbow as she sat down and handed her a napkin once she was settled. He'd always been nice—at least, as nice as a demanding perfectionist running a billion-dollar operation could be. But this was more than nice. It was gallant. Courtly.

"About your resignation," he began.

"Let me guess: you can't accept it."

He stared for a moment and then started laughing, shaking his head as he did. "Okay, I *can* accept your resignation. I just don't want to."

Her temper began to rise. There was plenty of stuff she didn't want to do, but she did it anyway. Mr. Benedict Merrill could have a little rain fall into his life for once. "Look, I've been responsible for Javier for five years now. This job has allowed me to support him *and* save for his education. I don't regret it—any of it. But I've been planning this next step for a long time." She aimed her forefinger at him. "I'm entitled to it."

He hooked an elbow over his chairback, his gaze going heavy. "I've been waiting too. I had some stuff planned for you myself."

Her filthy imagination instantly went to one of the fantasies she'd had about him—but those probably weren't the kind of plans he was talking about.

But maybe a raise... or a promotion?

"Really? Like a promotion?" Damn. Too eager. She was supposed to be leaving, not showing any interest in staying.

"Something like that," he said cagily.

Well, that didn't clarify things.

"For the past five years," he went on, "Javier has come first for you—as he should have. But in a few months, I figured you'd be ready for something more challenging."

It did sound tempting. She liked working for him and there was plenty of room for advancement in the company. But...

But she'd still be attracted to him. And she'd still want to get free of his charity. No matter how great the promotion was, she'd be no further ahead than she was now.

"Thanks," she said. "I do appreciate the offer. But I need to go... somewhere not here."

He did his little head-tilt motion that he only seemed to use with her. At least, she'd never seen him do it with anyone else. Probably because it was too cute to be used when negotiating a business deal. "Why? Why do you need to leave?" He straightened up, his brows meeting. "Has someone hurt you? Been threatening you?"

Hello, alpha male. "What? No," she spluttered. "Threaten me? Who would threaten me?"

His frown eased into something more solemn. "Is it me? Is it something I did?"

She rolled her eyes. "Not to get too clichéd, but it's not you, it's me. This job has been great and I really appreciate the opportunity you've given me... but all the opportunities I've ever had have come from your family. I went to college on the Merrill Family Memorial Scholarship. Most of the jobs here—at least the good ones—are at this ranch." She pressed her lips together. "My mother was your housekeeper even."

Pilar had been taking Merrill money since before she could even remember. And she was ready to stop.

"She was my family's housekeeper," he corrected. "And we mourned her too."

But not as much as Pilar had. And still did.

"Even so." She stared at the empty wineglass in front of her, watching the light trapped in it.

"I should have guessed it was something like this," he muttered. "Look," he said more loudly, "what can I do to convince you to stay?"

"Nothing."

He caught her hand, rubbed his thumb across her knuckles. Whoa. Grabbing her hand, clasping her elbow... He'd never before been so physical with her. Too bad she liked it so much, the heat of his hand, the largeness of it. A hand that big could easily cup her breasts...

Whoa. Whoa. Way too far.

"How about persuading? Could I do that?" he purred. Unlike before, there was no mistaking that for anything but a purr. Who knew the man could do such a thing?

"Um..." She licked her lips. *Focus, Pilar.* "I was going to finish my CPA certification."

Great. Way to kill the mood. Because what was sexier than an accountant?

"And I won't stop you."

God, his gaze was hot. What had they been talking about? It was so hard to remember, with his thumb rubbing across her knuckles like that. Almost as if he *wanted* to distract her.

The door opened. She squealed and tossed his hand away as if it were a black widow that had crawled across hers.

Hank, one of the steakhouse waiters, watched them warily from the doorway. "Should I come back?"

Benedict hooked his elbow over his chair once more, looking as if he'd never tried to distract her with that hand-caressing business. Or as if he didn't care Hank had caught him at it.

"No, we're ready," he said, easy like Sunday morning. "Pilar's hungry, aren't you?"

She was, but she wasn't supposed to admit that. She took half a second to frown at Benedict, then turned to smile at Hank. "Thank you. What did you bring us?"

He slid a plate in front of her, and the familiar smell nearly made her moan with pleasure.

"Carnitas," Hank said. "And here are your tortillas. Freshly made." He slid the same thing in front of Benedict, then disappeared again.

Pilar pondered her plate, the spicy scent of chilies tickling her nose. These carnitas would be hot enough to bring tears to her eyes, just like she liked them.

"What's wrong?" Benedict asked. "Why aren't you eating?"

"Oh, carnitas are a little messy." Any greasy, red spatters

that landed on the cream silk of her blouse would never come out.

He rose, a small frown pulling at his lips. Damn, but that was cute. He snatched up a napkin from the sideboard and stalked to her. His gaze was tight on hers as his hands slipped beneath the neckline of her blouse, tucking the napkin deeply into her cleavage, the backs of his hands hot against her bare skin. Did he even realize what he was doing?

She couldn't do anything *but* realize, her skin pebbling, her breasts going heavy and tight.

"There." He stepped back, studied his handiwork. Or her tits, which were in the same general direction. "Now you're all safe."

Safe? She felt like she was about to combust.

He settled back into his chair. "Eat your dinner," he ordered cheerfully. And then he winked at her.

He *did* know what he was doing.

Wait—what was he doing? Trying to convince her to stay? Or trying to seduce her?

This wasn't sexual harassment territory—this was the blank edge of the map labeled "Here be monsters."

She scooped some carnitas into a tortilla and took a big bite—partly because she *was* hungry and it smelled amazing and partly to have some time to think of something to say.

Spicy, savory, the tortilla carrying a hint of butter—God, these were good carnitas. Not quite as good as her madre's, but considering Pilar would never eat those particular carnitas again in this life, it would do.

"Good?" he asked, his smile treading dangerously close to a smirk. But a hot smirk. One that made her want to kiss it off his face.

She'd spent the past year being so good, trying so hard not to think about how goddamn sexy he was—and now he insisted that she couldn't leave, tucked her napkin into her cleavage, and fed her carnitas—*now* she couldn't think about anything but jumping his bones.

She was a bad feminist.

She nodded in response to his question, then swallowed. "So, about my resignation..."

His smile faded into sternness. And maybe a hint of... sadness? Yes, there, around his eyes.

"You're right, I can't stop you," he said, his voice lowering. "And I understand that you want to finish your certification now that Javier will be on his own."

"Well, Javier won't really be on his own," she corrected. "Even once he's at college, he'll still need me for stuff."

The twist of his mouth was skeptical. "Javier's not gonna want you fussing over him all the time. He'll have to learn to stand on his own two feet."

"Well, of course I know that. But if he needs me, I have to be there."

"Has he decided on a school?"

Javier had refused to even discuss sending out applications with her, but she wouldn't admit that. Couldn't bear to think that all the sacrifices she'd made over the years would be wasted if her brother didn't go to college.

And her parents? What would they have said if they'd known Javier might not get a college degree? They'd been so proud when she'd been accepted to UC Riverside. Surely they would want the same thing for Javier.

She was going to make certain he got it. Whether he wanted it right now or not. He'd thank her later.

"Not yet," she hedged. "But soon. And then I can finish my certification."

He dropped his gaze to his finger, which was tapping against the handle of his knife. "It's just—I thought you were happy here."

Spoken as if her leaving had any bearing on his future happiness. Really, she'd been a good admin, but she hadn't been *that* good.

"I am happy. But now I'm ready for something more."

Crap. She should have said *different*, something *different*. Because *more* implied that this job wasn't enough, that she was ungrateful. Even if she was ready for something more.

His gaze turned a darker shade of intense. She really was going to combust if he kept looking at her like that. "You know," he said thoughtfully, "if you're so determined to leave, I think we both might be ready for something more."

The heat flooding her face had nothing to do with the carnitas and everything to do with the wicked images she couldn't hold back. "What... what do you mean by more?"

But she knew. Oh God, she knew—the two of them, sweaty and entangled in a bed, her bent over his desk, her bare ass exposed—

It was all there in his heavy gaze, the intent, almost predatory set of his limbs, even in the rasp of his breath.

He wanted her too.

"What do you think I mean by more?" he asked, his gaze hot but his voice steadily neutral.

Was this a trap? She'd admit all the filthy things she wanted to do to him—the really filthy things she wanted him to do to her—and then he'd shout, "Psych!"

But that wasn't Benedict's MO.

"Well," she said carefully, "we've had a good working relationship—"

"I know," he said. "I've been there for it. I'm not talking about our working relationship. I'm talking about *more*."

Her limbs went still even as she shivered beneath her skin. "You mean a more—intimate relationship?"

Oh God, she didn't even dare to hope that was what he meant, except that she totally did.

He leaned in, dropped his voice. "It would have been unprofessional of us to do anything *intimate* while you were working for me," he answered. "But now that you're leaving..."

She released a slow breath into the silence coming on the trail of that. Was that what she wanted? A fling? With... *Benedict*?

Of course she wanted it. The real question was, did she dare say yes to him?

She looked him up and down, dark brown hair falling into his face, his tanned skin and the lines etched there speaking to a life spent as much out of doors as in an office. The open collar of his plain white button-down shirt, exposing a hint of his lean chest. And the rest of it she could imagine only too well—hard belly under that shirt, the long legs stretched out under the table, his boots crossed at the ankle. She'd had five years to look at him—and now she wanted to *look* at him.

She licked her lips. "How can we keep working together if we're...?"

If we're fucking. They really shouldn't do this. Really, really shouldn't.

But wasn't forbidden fruit the sweetest of all? She couldn't say, never having bitten into something as forbidden as banging the boss.

"If you think it's a bad idea," Benedict said, back to his usual seriousness, "you can say no. If you don't want to do it, say no. And we'll forget this ever happened." His hand tightened on hers. "If you say yes... Well, no matter what we do in private, we'll carry on just as before in the office."

He would do it too—she'd never seen so much as a hint of his personal life. No girlfriends, no orders for her to buy presents when he had no time—it was almost as if he had no intimate life.

Of course he had a personal life. It was clear he loved his siblings and parents. He was no corporate robot. He'd just never seemed to be dating anyone.

"Would we be dating?" she asked. "Or would this be secret?"

"It'll be whatever you want it to be, especially considering your situation with Javier."

Tempting. It was so tempting her mouth was watering. There had been *encounters* over the years—nothing serious since her brother occupied most of her life—but to have Benedict Merrill at her beck and call... her intimate, sexual beck and call...

It sounded amazing. "Have you been attracted to me this entire time?" she asked weakly.

"Yep."

Not even a hint of hesitation. And he didn't lie.

All of her went tight and hot and she had to squirm, just to rub some of the edge off. *Way to knock me on my ass.*

The entire time she'd been mentally lusting after him, *he'd* been mentally lusting after her. The two of them stewing together in unconscious sexual tension. It gave her the shivers, thinking on it.

"What'll it be, Pilar?" Low and rough. Just like the sex would probably be.

She'd be gone in three months no matter what, off to start her new life, to carve out something just for herself.

If she said yes to him, she could snatch a little something

that was all her own before she even left. Could scratch that yearlong itch she'd had for him with no danger of an awkward aftermath.

"Sure. Why not?"

He started to laugh, and she couldn't help but to join in. She'd just accepted her boss's offer of a torrid affair with *Sure, why not?*

It was ridiculous—even she could see that.

"Do you want to keep it quiet?" he asked.

"It's probably for the best. There's Javier, and I'm—well, I'm not what you usually go out with."

The temperature of his gaze dropped several degrees. "And what do I usually go out with?"

She pulled back, thought on it. "Nobody. You usually go out with nobody." She gave voice to her last horrid suspicion. "This isn't about convincing me to stay, is it?"

He made a scoffing kind of growl. "I don't want you to leave, but give me a little more credit than to use sex to keep you around."

"But if it's really good sex?"

He started laughing again, then sobered after a moment. "I'm going to miss you."

She swallowed, shook off the grayness of his words. This was meant to be fun. A fling, a joyous tossing off. Not heavy and entangled and sad. "I'm not leaving tomorrow," she said lightly. "And we'll, uh, be seeing more of each other in the future."

His mouth stretched in a smile that made her want to melt into her chair. "Yes, we will," he agreed. "How do you want to work this? I'm guessing you can't stay the night."

She'd bet he had a California king with sheets made from handwoven silk. And his bathroom... his bathroom was probably palatial. She sighed. "No, I can't spend the night. Let me think of something." Of course, if Javier kept to his routine of not coming home most nights, she wouldn't need to be home either.

Which wouldn't stop her from waiting up for him. On that note, she flicked on her phone, checked the text messages.

Still nothing from her brother. Typical.

"I suppose I should head home," she said. Javier better be there waiting for her or...

Or what? You'll ground him?

Why had God made teenage boys so difficult? It was almost as if Javier wanted her to kick him out of the house. She grabbed her purse, glanced at Benedict.

What was she supposed to do now? Did she just say good-bye and walk out? Did she give him a kiss? They *were* on company property.

"I'll walk you to your car." He rose, and she had to appreciate just how tall he was. She knew of course, but if things went where they were supposed to, she'd be entwined with the length of him soon.

Get it together, Pilar. You're the one making this weird. He's totally cool.

He really was totally cool, holding the door for her as if this were nothing, as if he propositioned his assistant all the time.

All right, she could be cool too. Composed, professional, completely in control of the situation. She kept her eyes straight ahead, two feet of space between them. Her heels went click-click-click along the asphalt, in time with the deeper thunk of his boot heels.

"What happened to your old car?" he demanded when she stopped at her battered compact and shook out her keys.

Damn. She never had told him what happened. Likely because he was only her boss then. "Someone made an illegal turn in front of me, and the car was totaled. The insurance money would only pay for this."

"Jesus," he breathed. "Are you okay? Are you having nightmares?"

She heard what he left unsaid. *Because of what happened to your parents.*

"No. Like, I mean, I had a few, but I'm fine now." And she'd flinched for months whenever someone had turned left in front of her, but she'd sucked it up and kept on driving. It was that or walk.

"If you need to talk with someone, I'm happy to pay for it," he said gently.

"I have excellent mental health benefits, remember?"

He took the keys from her, opening the door for her as if he did it all the time. "If you need to see someone, promise me you'll do it."

Ha. After all the counselors she'd had to deal with in the foster care system as Javier's guardian, she had no desire to talk about her feelings ever again. "Oh, don't worry, I will. If I need it. See you tomorrow."

And then she waited. She couldn't say why—he wasn't going to kiss her. Anyone might see them if they did.

He leaned in, a hint of his aftershave touching her nose, sweetly tart. She licked her lips, wondering if his skin tasted the same.

They remained like that for a moment, nose to nose, the night and their wants heavy on them.

"We're on company property," she reminded him softly.

"Parking lot doesn't count."

His lips brushed hers, soft and slow, no hurry there. Only savoring as he did it again and again, as if he'd been dreaming of just their lips touching for forever. It was really... romantic.

No, this wasn't supposed to be romantic. He was already welching on the deal. She parted her lips and touched her tongue to his.

It was like she'd struck a match. His mouth grew greedy, demanding, and he grabbed two handfuls of her ass, pulling her hard against him. He growled or moaned—or growl-moaned—and pulled her up to cling to him, her skirt sliding up as her legs wrapped around his hips, her arms hanging around his neck as if he were her lifeline.

Oh God, with his mouth hungry on hers and her pussy rubbed up against his lower belly—and goddamn, he was growling again—it was the hottest kiss of her entire life. With her boss. In the parking lot at work.

His hands slid under her skirt, palms rough even through her tights. Her skirt gave a rather ominous rip.

"Careful," she muttered against his mouth. "My skirt."

"Fuck it. I'll buy you another one. I'll buy you fifty."

His hand kept sliding around, past her ass, along her inner thigh, and then—holy crap, he found her clit on the very first try. Through her panties *and* her tights.

The man was a god.

Now *she* was moaning and his finger began to circle— just right, oh just right—soon enough she'd be sobbing...

"I want to taste you so badly," he rasped into her ear. "I've dreamed about it."

She could imagine it, her lying on the seat of her car, him on his knees in this parking lot, his head between her thighs.

Crazy hot, that image. Or maybe just crazy.

"Wait," she muttered. "We can't... someone might come by." She unwrapped her legs from his hips, pushed against his shoulders, and he slid her down the length of him until her feet hit the pavement. With a wriggle and a shimmy, she jerked her skirt back into place.

It was going to take more than a wriggle and a shimmy to return him to respectability, judging by the hard bulge in the front of his Wranglers.

He watched her with an intent gaze. Then he did that romantic business again—he cupped her face in his hands and brushed another of those sweet kisses across her lips. "Will you be all right getting home?"

"Of course." She pulled out of his grasp, the gentleness of it somehow hurtful. "I do it every night."

He helped her into the car, bracing his arm against the door and leaning over her as she snapped on her seat belt. For a moment she feared he'd give her another kiss—feared it because she felt close to tears in a way she didn't like and didn't understand.

"Drive safely," he said. "Because I can't wait to see you tomorrow."

He shut the door. She watched him in the rearview mirror until the night and distance swallowed him, as he watched back, unmoving.

Chapter 3

TWO EGGS OR FOUR?

Pilar pondered that question for the ages as she stared at the open egg carton, the local morning DJs laughing like tinny hyenas from the radio on the sill above the kitchen sink.

If was just her, it would be two. If Javier deigned to eat, then it would be four.

Better go see what his breakfast plans were.

It hadn't been like this right after their parents had died —they'd clung to each other in the aftermath, her never wanting to leave Javier, him never wanting to leave her. He'd been thirteen; she'd been twenty-one. Way too young to suddenly be responsible for a teenager. Or to be an orphan. She'd called him Javi back then. She hadn't done that in a while now.

The call had come during finals week of her last quarter at UCR. She'd been in her apartment just off campus, studying for some final—she didn't remember which one.

But she remembered the trill of the phone breaking into her concentration, the way she'd flinched at the interruption. The long, long moments of Lupe simply sobbing into the phone after Pilar had answered.

The rest was blurred, jumpy. Getting home, taking charge of Javier, the funerals... so much she'd had to do and worry over in those first few weeks. No wonder her memory hadn't been able to hold on to most of it.

But there had been help. Their community had rallied around them, providing food and companionship and contacting relatives in Mexico. She and Javier had been orphans, but they'd never really been alone, thanks to her parents' friends.

She did remember Benedict taking charge of a lot of the official stuff in those terrible early weeks, his siblings helping. Somehow the funeral home was contacted, the Mass was scheduled, the flowers appeared—the cemetery plots had even been prescreened for her. She only had to pick out of two or three choices. And the lawyer who'd handled the settlement from the accident and the probate mess had been paid by the Merrills, thank God. She couldn't have afforded it and wasn't clear enough in her head then to pick a good lawyer anyway.

Marching into Benedict's office to beg for a job was her first real impression after the blur of her parents' deaths.

Things had come into sharp, clear focus that first Dia de los Muertos, when she'd laid Abuela Rosa's favorite bolillos on the ofrenda, followed by Tio Luis's favorite candies, just like her mother had. Then with shaking hands she'd set a jar of atole there for her father and some pink pan dulce for her mother, nestling them among the marigolds and candles, Javier watching silently as she had.

She'd kept a practiced smile on her face as the neighbors had come, bearing sugar skulls and pan de muerto, and reminiscing with her and Javier. But she'd only managed one bite of the pan de muerto, that bit sliding down her throat hard as a rock, because it hadn't tasted exactly like her mother's.

Her job, caring for Javier, keeping herself together... she'd survived that first year, thought maybe things were even going well the second year. She'd even managed several bites of pan de muerto on Dia de los Muertos that second year. But slowly she and Javier had moved forward into their present state of delightful noncommunication, despite her best efforts.

Her brother wasn't in his room, although he had come home last night—she'd heard him moving around when she'd come home, although he hadn't come out to greet her. It was the usual mess of clothes and papers and car magazines. And the *smell*. He showered every day—she had the water bill to prove it—so why did his room smell like this?

She did her best to make her way through, picking up clothes as she went. Were they clean? Were they dirty? Who could tell? She tossed an armful into the hall to wash later, then went back for the mountain of clothes on top of his dresser.

That's when she noticed the work pants. Three pairs, tags still on, an expensive brand.

She picked them up, the heavy fabric rough in her hands. Where had he gotten the money for these?

"What are you doing in here?"

She spun at Javier's voice behind her, holding in her flinch of surprise. It was her house, he was under her guidance—she had every right to be in his room.

"Looking for you." Her fingers tightened on the pants. Should she ask him about them?

No, not now. She didn't want to fight this morning.

They'd save their fight for this afternoon when they met with the school guidance counselor.

"What do you want?" As sullen and slouchy as ever. Their mother would have been appalled by his attitude.

Sometimes Pilar was almost grateful her parents couldn't see what a mess she was making of things. "Do you want some eggs?"

His dark hair fell into his face, hiding his brown eyes. "I guess." He shrugged, as if the flatness of his tone hadn't already told her how little he cared.

"I can cook up some machaca too."

"Whatever."

On that sparkling note, he turned and left.

She caught up with him in the kitchen, where he was chugging a tall glass of orange juice.

Four eggs into the pan. And some machaca as well. She hummed along to the radio as she watched them cook. This had been their mother's favorite song. Pilar remembered singing along to the corrido with her in this very kitchen, her mother's voice filling the room—

The music cut off with a smack.

"What the—"

Javier's palm was on the off button, a grimace on his face. "I can't listen to that shit this early in the morning. And where were you last night?"

"I had a late meeting with Benedict." She would not blush. She would not blush...

"You weren't here when I got home," he whined, "and I didn't have any dinner."

"I didn't see you when I got home. And you never texted me back."

He flopped into a chair. "I went to bed. Hungry."

She remembered Benedict's irritation at Javier not

feeding himself, felt an echo of it clench her own jaw. "And you couldn't fix something for yourself? It's all on me?"

"I didn't feel like it."

That was the problem. Javier never felt like doing anything anymore. "You're old enough to make your own dinner," she snapped. "What will you do at school when the cafeteria is closed?"

"Unggghh. God, don't start on that."

Panic mixed in with her irritation and began to eat at her stomach. She dished out the eggs onto a plate, resisting the urge to smack him across the face with the spatula. "Have you heard back from any schools yet?" She slid the plate in front of him, flattening her voice into something closer to chipper. "They should be sending out letters soon."

"No, and I don't want to talk about it." He scooped up the eggs with his tortilla, shoveled his mouth full of food, and chewed noisily.

"Okay." *Don't push too hard. He'll just shut down.* "We can talk about it at our meeting with Ms. Ramirez today. Don't forget."

"I know," he mumbled. "I'll be there, okay?"

As if her concern for him was oh so burdensome.

She slapped the spatula onto the counter. "Will you? Because some nights you don't come home and don't bother to tell me. What are you doing then?"

"Don't worry about it. It's none of your business."

"The hell it isn't. What's going on with you?"

"Nothing!" He shoved his plate away and snapped to his feet. "I said don't worry about it. And stop asking about stupid college. That's all I ever get from you—you busting my balls."

Her worries about his future, her sacrifices to ensure

that future was bright—that was *busting his balls*? "I pinched and scrimped and starved to build your college fund."

"Well, maybe I don't want to go." He crossed his arms, looking like a toddler about to start screaming.

No. He had to go to college. He wasn't letting all of them —her, their parents—down like that. "So I saved all that money for nothing?"

"I never asked you to save that money."

She put the heels of her hands to her eyes, rubbed hard. "What am I going to do with you?"

"Do with me?" He threw his arms wide. "Do you even hear yourself? I'm not some stupid project at work," he snarled.

He stomped out, slamming the door hard. There was a crash from the hallway, the sharp chime of breaking glass echoing in the silence.

Wonderful. Just fucking wonderful. That was probably the family portrait that had fallen—the last one taken of all four of them.

She sat at the kitchen table, folded her arms, and rested her head in the comforting darkness she'd created there.

The creak of the front door opening had her raising her head. Javier slumped back into the kitchen.

"Forgot my backpack," he mumbled.

"Oh." She sniffled and wiped her nose. "Well, go get it. Don't want to be late for school."

Avoidance, aversion, sweeping it all away to deal with later, although later never came—she couldn't keep dealing with him this way. But she was so tired of trying to reach him, and nothing else was working.

He waited, his fists clenched by his sides. "I'm sorry about the picture." Defiant, as if daring her to reject his apology. But at least he'd apologized. "I'll go clean it up."

She blinked. The offer was almost as shocking as his apology. "Thanks," she said, her voice weak.

He shuffled to the broom closet, returned with the broom, and soon enough the sounds of cleanup came from the hallway.

She tried to eat her cold eggs and to pretend that things weren't very, very wrong between them.

The rest of the morning passed without incident until she got to work. She parked the car, grabbed her purse, slammed the door... and stopped dead.

There was a bulge in the tire.

Her skin washed in clammy tension as she imagined the tire blowing, the car veering toward a concrete median as she desperately tried to stop it—

No. No, now was not the time to think about that. She was here. She'd survived. And she'd get the tire fixed.

But probably not before the meeting with Ms. Ramirez today. Maybe she could get a ride from someone. Who'd be home around that time? Lupe—she was working the night shift at the hospital this week, so she could drop Pilar off on her way to work.

There remained the problem of how to get home after, but she'd worry about it later. Along with the problem of getting a new tire. She didn't have a spare—in a fit of stupidity, she'd decided not to buy one, figuring that if something happened, she could buy one off Ignacio. He always had tires to sell.

And now she was looking at spending hundreds for a new tire and a tow, all to save a fraction of that on a spare tire. So dumb of her. She rubbed at her forehead. No time to cry. She had to call Lupe and then get her butt behind her desk—

"You didn't drive on that?"

She spun around to find Benedict glaring at her. "I won't again," she bit off, her heart jumping with surprise. "I didn't check before I left."

He crouched beside the tire to inspect it, his big hands running over the rubber tread, his shirt stretching tight across the expanse of his back. Her heart kept on being jumpy.

"You have to check before you leave."

"I know that now." Did he have to be so smug about it? Although he didn't really sound smug. More like concerned.

He looked up from the tire, and something like pain flickered in his gaze. "Sorry. I just about had a heart attack seeing this tire and knowing you'd been driving on it."

Well, that made her feel like crap, having snapped at him. "I'll get it fixed before I drive it home." When that would be, she wasn't sure, but he didn't need to know that.

"I'll have it fixed." He stood and pulled a handkerchief from his pocket, scrubbing the black marks from his hands with it.

"Wait, no— This was supposed—" She dropped her voice. "This was supposed to only be in private. Not you publicly buying me tires!"

He raised an eyebrow. "It's only a tire. Although you should replace all four of them. And get the front end aligned."

And drop a grand into this rust bucket? No.

He held up a hand when her mouth pinched up. "I'll take it out of your salary, okay?"

"You can't do that." More charity. How could she refuse his offer without looking like an ungrateful brat?

She couldn't.

"Buy you tires?" he asked. "Or take it out of your salary?"

"Any of it. And stuff like this—" She flailed at the car. "People like you don't mess around with cars."

"Actually, I change all the fluids on my truck and do most of the maintenance myself. My father taught me how. It's a good skill to have."

She wouldn't admit how appealing that made him. Her father had done all the maintenance and repairs on their cars. Javier had inherited her father's skills with an engine—too bad he hadn't bothered to check her tires before this had happened.

And now Benedict wanted to fix it.

She crossed her arms over her chest. Mostly to keep herself from saying yes to his offer. Because it sounded nice, just handing over the whole mess and letting him deal with it. Knowing Benedict, he'd have four new tires on it by lunchtime.

"I can handle it myself," she said. God, she sounded like Javier.

"Hey." He placed a hand on her forearm, the heat of his skin reassuring. "I know you can. But I want to help."

She wanted to say no to that help. For once. But this time she was in a serious bind. "Well..." She nibbled on her lip and he gave her arm a small squeeze. One that said *Trust me.* "Okay. But only because I have to meet Javier's guidance counselor today. And you will have the bill sent to me."

"Fair enough." He took his hand from her arm and picked her purse up from the asphalt. "And I'll drive you to the meeting."

She started to protest but caught herself. If he were taking care of the tires, what did it matter if he drove her too?

"Okay. Thanks."

Her plan to disentangle herself from Benedict Merrill's

charity was going just swimmingly. If her plan to have a fling with him went as badly...

She was definitely leaving in three months. The fling would be over, and she'd never get another handout from him after that. Problem solved.

Her morning was spent at her desk, dealing with e-mails and filing and such. Benedict was at the stockyards, saving her from the awkwardness of having to work alongside him after discovering that he wanted her as much as she wanted him.

And the knowledge that they would do something about that wanting would be rubbing between them as they tried to concentrate on business... Nope, much better that Benedict was gone.

She was deep in an expense report when he came back, climbing through receipts and credit statements as she tried to make sense of it.

He set a hip against her desk and gave her a slow, lazy smile. "Hey."

"Hey yourself." She smiled back.

No. Wait. They were supposed to be professional about this. But how could she resist when he looked like that?

"I've ordered us some lunch," he said, his voice a pleasant rumble. "It should be here soon, so finish up."

"Oh"—she dropped the expense report, grabbed the drawer handle—"I have a—"

"A peanut butter sandwich, I know." His lips twitched with suppressed laughter. "Don't you want a change?"

How did he know she ate a peanut butter sandwich every day?

Hank wheeled in a catering tray. "In your office, boss?"

"Yep." Benedict pushed off from her desk. "Finish up," he ordered her.

Maybe he just wanted to work through lunch. In which case, she *had* to go eat with him. It being part of her job and all that.

It was only lunch. Benedict wasn't going to seduce her over sandwiches in his office. Not that she wanted him to. That particular fantasy needed to stay safely in her head. But again, no danger of that happening.

Right?

Only one way to find out.

She walked into Benedict's office to find Hank gone and two heaping salads on the catering cart, each topped with a generous serving of seared ahi, so deeply pink they were closer to ruby.

How could she say no to go eat a peanut butter sandwich?

Benedict of course knew that she couldn't. Which was why he was smirking at her right now.

"Was there something you wanted to work on over lunch?" she asked pointedly.

"Nope." His smile deepened. "Just you and me, having a conversation. I really like talking to you, by the way."

She plopped into a chair, took the plate he offered her. Well. She couldn't be snippy when he said things like that. "Thank you," she said primly.

He settled across from her, looking much easier than she felt, and tucked in to his salad. "Was Javier there when you got home?"

She frowned. She didn't remember telling him that Javier wasn't coming home regularly. "Of course he was."

"Oh. Because you kept checking your text messages with a worried look on your face."

She'd have to get better at hiding her reactions from

him. Or else he might figure out what was really up with her brother.

"Nope, he was there. Safe and sound." She shoved enough lettuce in her mouth to choke a horse. That ought to stop any more questions from him.

"How's Javier doing?"

Like that one.

Her first instinct was to lie. To say that everything was just perfect, that he was falling right in with all her plans for him to go to college, that all the money she'd saved was going to be used for exactly what it should be. That the efforts of the past five years had not at all been in vain.

But she was also getting tired of lying. Of pretending that she was on the ball and not a complete failure at rearing a teenager.

Had it been a relief for Benedict in some way when Josh had finally gone to prison, to not have to pretend anymore that everything was fine? She didn't know; he never spoke of Josh. At least not to her.

It seemed rather silly to be ashamed of what was happening with Javier when Josh's situation was much, much worse.

"I don't know what to do with him," she admitted. "He refuses to discuss college, he's sullen, he... some nights he doesn't even come home." She flipped over a piece of tuna, the pink of it jewel bright against the green lettuce. Almost too bright to be real.

Benedict didn't say anything. Maybe he was shocked by that. Maybe he was pissed she'd been lying all this time.

Or maybe he wasn't surprised. Maybe he'd suspected this all along.

"When Josh was having trouble..." His voice went rough. "I tried everything I could think of and nothing worked."

God, she knew how that felt. She could sing that song word for word.

Josh had been blackout drunk—just like the driver who'd killed her parents—when he'd wrapped his Ferrari around a telephone pole, almost killing himself and his girlfriend. He'd gotten six years for drunk driving. His prison sentence had started right before her parents had died.

Benedict had been so grim in those early months it had almost frightened her. But he'd never been mean or short with her as she'd wandered through her own grief. Slowly, they'd both grown into their working relationship.

Now here they were. Sharing lunch. And their worries about their younger brothers.

"It wasn't your fault," she said. "You couldn't have stopped him." Any more than she was able to stop Javier.

He stirred through his salad but didn't take a bite. "I still feel responsible on some level. Dad was having heart problems, I'd just taken over most of his role in the company—I felt like I should have straightened out Josh too."

"How are your parents?" She didn't really know Mr. Merrill, but Mrs. Merrill had always been nice to her.

"Enjoying their retirement. I never thought Dad would slow down, but I guess Cambria is pretty enough for even him to notice."

She smiled. "He knows he left the family business in good hands."

Benedict shook his head. "Couldn't fix what was wrong with Josh. At least not before he ended up in prison."

She pondered what to say next, because this was tricky territory. Given what had happened to her own parents, she definitely believed Josh had gotten what he'd deserved.

But he was also Benedict's brother.

"Josh is coming home soon, isn't he?" she asked carefully.

He nodded. "Yeah. In six months." He turned his water glass in circles, never picking it up. Just endlessly turning it to nowhere.

"How's he doing?"

Benedict jerked his shoulders in a shrug, but he wasn't a shrugging kind of guy. The carelessness of the gesture looked foreign on him. "He, uh, he didn't want me to visit. Liliana visits him, though. She says he's doing okay."

If Javier said he didn't want to see her anymore... She swallowed, the sound echoing wetly in her ears. "I'm sorry. I shouldn't have said anything."

He released the glass and looked at her, his gaze stark. "No, it's okay. You're the only person outside of family to talk about Josh with me in a long time. Everyone else acts as if he's dead. Out of sight, out of mind and all that."

His expression made her feel raw, inside out. Who knew he'd been hiding all that for so long?

"But he's not out of your mind."

"No."

So firm, so definite. She knew then that no matter what Josh had done, no matter that he'd turned Benedict away, Benedict would never stop caring.

She reached over and took his hand, because he shouldn't be alone admitting this. Not when she felt the same about her own little brother. He turned his hand over so that their palms met, their fingers curling around each other as if carved to fit.

They took a long moment like that, just holding on to each other. She didn't feel the need to talk, nor did she need him to say anything. It was better in the silence, this new understanding between them.

After a time, he gave her hand a quick squeeze, then pulled away. She let her lips twist briefly at the loss, but that was all. Time to return to their professional roles.

"The salad is really good," she offered. "Thanks for thinking of it."

"You're welcome. I'm glad you like it." When he smiled, there wasn't any heat in it—it was friendly, open, *happy*. It warmed her all over.

When they'd finished up and stacked the plates onto the catering cart for Hank, he glanced at his watch. "What time is your meeting today?"

"I have to be at the high school at three thirty."

He slowly lowered his forearm, his movements taking on a deliberateness that made all of her come to attention. "And how long do you have for lunch?" he asked, slow and sultry as a Sunday afternoon in July.

"An hour." Oh, she was already all breathy and twitchy. What was he up to? Or was he up to anything?

He slipped the watch from his wrist, setting the heavy gold band onto his desk with a weighty thump. "You have ten more minutes off the clock then."

She stared at the watch face looking back at her, watching as the hand swept away the seconds. "Yes. But—"

"Sit down." Not quite a command from him—just enough force there to make her breath hitch.

She found her way to her usual chair, the one across from his desk, the one she always sat in as she took his orders. The watch stared sightlessly back at her.

"Do you want me to...?" She kept her gaze on the watch as she let that question fade between them, feeling him prowling behind her.

He set his hands on the arms of her chair, the bulk of

him at her back, his mouth coming close to her ear. All of her prickled with his nearness.

"Tell me when your ten minutes is up," he said with pleasant menace.

She pressed her knees hard together, trying to keep her desire contained. "You can't—We're in your office."

"I won't touch you. And in ten minutes, you'll go back to your desk."

There was a metallic scrape. His belt buckle, rubbing against the back of her chair.

What could he possibly do to her in ten minutes? Without touching her?

God, but she wanted to know. Her toes curled in her shoes.

"Watch the clock," he ordered, low and harsh, his breath hot against her neck. "Wouldn't want to steal any company time."

His fingers tightened on the arms of the chair, and she could almost feel his fingertips sinking into her flesh. Right there on her upper thighs, gripping her tight, holding her open for him...

He didn't even have to do anything. Her own filthy imagination was doing all the work.

He blew on the exposed skin of her neck, drawing a line from the tendon of her shoulder all the way to her neck, hot and humid.

"Oh Jesus," she moaned, every muscle clenching tight.

He laughed, soft and deep. "I wish that had been my tongue. Don't you?"

She whimpered. Okay, she'd been wrong. He was going to do a hell of a lot in just ten minutes without even touching her.

He repeated his breath trick on the other side and her

breasts tightened, nipples coming to hard points. But she knew he wasn't going to cup them, wasn't going to rub away the torment building there, and that made it so much worse.

She could feel him behind her, hovering over her. He could probably look right down her shirt like that, might even see the lace edging of her bra, black as sin.

"I like your lingerie," he said.

Her eyes dipped closed. He was good. So good. His fingers would dip beneath that black lace, slip down to find her nipples—

"How much time left?" he asked.

She forced her eyes open, tried to focus on the watch.

"Six minutes," she got out finally.

"Mmm."

She couldn't tell if he was annoyed or pleased. All she knew was that one little noise of his seemed to have lodged in her midsection and shaken her.

He leaned over her shoulder, the strands of his dark hair filling her peripheral vision. She kept her gaze hard on the watch and went still.

She could reach up and stroke his hair if she wanted. Which she did. Very badly. And he was more than close enough to touch her. *Accidentally.*

Would he?

He directed a caressing stream of breath right down her shirt, finally touching her breasts. She arched back, searching for more. But it wasn't enough—she slipped her foot from her shoe, rubbed her arch along her calf, needing something, anything to keep from dying of need.

"Christ," he muttered.

It was what she would have said, had she been able to speak, and it proved he was just as caught up in this as she.

That, along with the rasp of his breathing in her ear, his lungs working as hard as hers.

She hooked her foot around her calf, held tight, needing something to anchor her if he wasn't going to touch her. He swallowed hard behind her, his fingers so tight on the arms of the chair that his knuckles were bone white.

"Pilar." Harder than a whisper, softer than a demand— he made her name into an imprecation.

"Yes?" Ragged. Needy.

And then the phone rang.

His arms framing her went taut and long as he leaned away. "Fuck," he sighed under his breath.

She blinked at the watch, twisted to look up at him. "But we still have four minutes."

The roar of his laughter twined with the insistent trill of the phone. He sobered and wiped at his eyes. "Duty calls." He sounded as if he'd rather do anything but answer that phone.

"I'll just let you get that then." She stood on wobbly legs, feeling as if she'd downed too much champagne way too fast.

As she made her way back to her desk, she realized that these next three months were going to be much more interesting than she'd ever imagined.

Chapter 4

BENEDICT HAD A REALLY NICE TRUCK.

Pilar ran her hands along the leather of the seat and admired the walnut trim of the console. Who knew they made luxury trucks?

He'd hauled hay in it recently though. The sweetly dry smell of it tickled her nose even now.

Benedict's truck was just like his life—a mixture of orderly luxury and rugged functionality. He certainly kept the truck cabin as clean and clutter-free as his office was. No doubt the interior of her car would give him fits.

She glanced over at him, his hands firm on the wheel, gaze straight on the road. He hadn't said much as they made their way to the high school, which she appreciated. Drivers who didn't pay enough attention to the road made her nervous.

Plus she could keep sneaking glances at him like a creeper without freaking him out too much. She liked looking at him openly like this. No need to hide her want anymore.

That one pesky hunk of hair had fallen across his forehead, but he hadn't bothered to push it back. His eyes were hidden behind his sunglasses, but the flat line of his mouth spoke to his focus on driving.

Maybe, after what Josh had done, he didn't like it when people didn't pay enough attention to the road too.

His confessions at lunch had been so intimate. Almost more intimate than his little game of "no touching" after. Had he ever shared those feelings with his siblings? Or was she the first person he'd ever shown them to?

She had the feeling he hadn't said anything to Liliana or Luke. They probably guessed at Josh's rejection and Benedict's hurt—they weren't stupid—but Benedict likely hadn't openly confessed what had happened. He would want to appear strong, unflappable, to his younger siblings.

That was certainly how she wanted to appear to Javier. As if she actually knew what she was doing in all this.

She sighed as they pulled up to a stoplight. She had no clue what she was doing, and in about fifteen minutes, the career counselor was going to realize that as well.

Maybe Ms. Ramirez could convince Javier of the importance of college. Or at least get him to discuss the idea.

"What's this meeting about?" Benedict asked. He kept his eyes on the road, even though they were stopped.

"All the graduating seniors and their parents meet with the career counselor to talk about their future plans." She brought her thumbnail to her mouth and started to worry at it. What would Javier say at this meeting? That he didn't want to talk about his future plans?

Lord, the counselor was going to think they were a dysfunctional wreck of a family.

"What did you tell the counselor when you were graduating?" he asked.

"Oh, that I was going to major in Latin American history." She laughed. "Of course, after the first quarter I realized I should pick something that actually gave me a chance of getting a job."

"So you left behind Latin American history for the glamour of accounting?"

"I enjoy accounting. There's something very satisfying about organizing account information and money flow." She gestured as if to organize an imaginary spreadsheet, a warm glow sparking in her. "I'm bringing order to what most people would leave as chaos."

He nodded. "Yep. I like order too."

"Yeah, I can tell from your truck. And your office."

"I like things to be in their place. Their proper place." He flicked a glance toward her, and she wished the sunglasses were gone so that she might read his expression.

Did he mean that her proper place was as his secretary?

Or something more?

The light changed and his focus returned to driving.

She let out a silent breath. It had been nothing. Only her imagination. "I didn't leave Latin American history behind," she said. "I kept it as my minor. I thought then that I could have everything I wanted out of life if I just reached for it."

He made a sad sort of exhale. "That's the trouble with getting older: you realize everything isn't yours for the asking."

She agreed, but—"I don't mean to be bitchy or to suggest that you don't have problems, but what do you want that you can't have?"

A long, tense silence. "There's something I've wanted for a long time that I'm starting to suspect I'll never have." Grim. Just skirting the border of despair.

Her skin tightened as goosebumps rose all over. He didn't mean her. He said he wanted her and she'd agreed to this secret affair. That was the exact opposite of him not getting what he wanted.

Before she could figure it out, they were pulling into the high school parking lot. And there was Javier, looking just *delighted* to be waiting for her.

This meeting was going to be an utter disaster.

Her seat belt released with a sharp click, and she looked down in surprise to find Benedict unbuckling it for her.

"Stay where you are," he warned her. "I'm coming around to get the door for you."

"Oh, but you don't need to—"

He raised his eyebrow.

She closed her mouth.

Watching him stalk around the front of the truck as he went for her door made flutters dance in her stomach. His caveman act was surprising—and surprisingly hot. He'd never insisted on such a thing before, but he'd also never played sexy head games with her in the office before either.

He swung the door open and held a hand out to her.

"I'm beginning to think I don't know you very well at all," she said wonderingly, slipping her hand into his.

"Just figuring that out, huh?" The left corner of his mouth quirked up, putting a dent of a dimple into his cheek. "Think three months is enough now?"

She was beginning to suspect it wasn't. Which was a very bad thing.

"Where's your car?" Javier had come over and was scowling.

"The tire had a bulge." She pulled her hand from Benedict's, both her feet now safely on the ground.

Javier sneered as he looked at Benedict. "So your boss brought you? Nice." He made it sound anything but nice.

Benedict's jaw tensed, but he kept quiet.

"Javier," she hissed, "watch it."

"What? I said it was nice."

"I'll just wait in the truck." Benedict did not sound happy.

"Really," she said, "you don't have to—"

Both his eyebrows went up.

She sighed. "We should be done in about an hour."

As they trudged toward the office, she asked, "How was your day?"

Javier didn't answer, only slumped over as if his backpack were filled with bricks.

Great. This meeting was going to be just *great.* She gritted her teeth and reached for the office door handle.

"Why is he driving you?"

She blinked in surprise at that outburst from her brother. "I told you, the tire had a bulge. I couldn't drive on it."

"So Mr. Big Shot drove you here 'cause he's such a nice guy?" Caustic enough to burn her ears.

No, he drove me because I told him I wanted to fuck him.

"I didn't have time to get the tire fixed, and I wanted to be sure I made this meeting," she said, intent and deliberate. Javier needed to snap out of this right this instant.

"Who's fixing the tire?" he demanded.

Oh, so now he cared? Maybe he should have cared before she'd left for work this morning. "I don't know. Benedict's got someone doing it."

"Benedict," he sneered under his breath.

"Knock it off," she snapped. "I don't know what your problem is, but we need to get to this meeting."

He just shrugged.

She dug her knuckles into her forehead for a second,

then dropped her hand, shook herself. Javier's pissiness couldn't get to her. She had to look competent here.

Ms. Ramirez was waiting for them, looking as tired as Pilar felt. No wonder—the poor woman had to spend her day interacting with hundreds of teenagers. Just dealing with the one was more than enough for Pilar.

"Javier. Pilar." She smiled warmly as she gestured them into her office. It was the same one she'd been in when Pilar had been in high school. But this meeting would be a lot different than her last one with Ms. Ramirez. No scholarship for Javier, no acceptance to any schools. And no parents beaming proudly at him.

Just Pilar doing her best and failing miserably.

"How are you, Ms. Ramirez?" She smiled and shook the counselor's hand.

"Good. And don't you look well."

"Thank you." Pilar gave herself half a moment to internally preen, because she really did look good in these pants.

"So," Ms. Ramirez began, "we're here to discuss Javier's plans for after graduation. I understand that you want him to apply to some colleges—"

"Tell her I don't want to go," Javier cut in, his voice thin and high.

Surprised silence.

"Javier," Pilar began, her tone cajoling, "I don't think you've thought this through." She knew he hadn't. Otherwise he'd have already picked a school.

"How would you know? You won't listen to me. About anything."

"You won't talk!" This was *not* her fault.

"Let's take a step back," Ms. Ramirez said.

"Yes, let's." Pilar glared at Javier. Stupid, stupid boy. "Okay, so you don't go to college. What do you do then? Mop floors? Pick in the fields? Our parents worked too long and hard—and you're going to toss all that away?"

"See?" He threw a pleading glance at Ms. Ramirez as he shoved a hand at Pilar. "She throws our parents at me every time."

"Throw them at you? I just want for you what they wanted for you."

"How do you know what they wanted for me?"

"But they wanted me to go to college," she said. "They were so happy about it." Why wouldn't they want the same for Javier?

"I'm not you." Defiant. Sullen. His attitude was back to square one.

Ms. Ramirez held her hands up for silence. "Perhaps we should try another tack—"

"Yes." Pilar nodded enthusiastically. Perhaps the counselor knew of another way to convince Javier of how important college was.

"—and let's shelve the college discussion for now," Ms. Ramirez finished.

Pilar's head stopped midnod. What? Not talk about college?

"Good," Javier huffed. "'Cause I'm not going."

She turned on him, ready to launch into a tirade.

"Ah." Ms. Ramirez waggled her finger at her.

Okay. No more college talk. Fine. She could do that. "So," she asked her brother, "what will you do instead?"

He dropped his head and shrugged. "I don't know."

She stared at him for a long time, not caring that Ms. Ramirez was there.

I don't know.

All that money sitting in the bank, thousands and thousands of dollars—five years of *her life*—and he didn't know what he was going to be doing in three months? Or for the rest of his life?

He should have punched her right in the chest—that would have been less shocking. Would have hurt less.

"Javier, that's not really an answer," Ms. Ramirez said gently.

He just shrugged again, his face averted as if he might cry.

Pilar felt as if she might cry too. And tired. She was so, so tired.

Ms. Ramirez's deep sigh seemed to capture all the sadness and exhaustion floating between Pilar and her brother. "Let's try this again later. Javier, you come up with an answer for your sister. And Pilar, you be ready to listen. Really listen."

She did listen. She always listened. Javier wouldn't talk.

"All right," she agreed. "If Javier has an answer, I'll listen. Without arguing."

Javier made a noise of disbelief.

She ignored him, held her hand out to Ms. Ramirez. "Thank you for seeing us. I'm sorry it wasn't more productive."

Javier ignored her as they left the office, veering off the opposite direction when they reached the parking lot.

"Where are you going?" she called after him. "Benedict's truck is this way."

"I know where it is." He didn't turn back.

"Then where are you going?" Was there once, just once, where he could behave normally and not like the world's most stereotypical teenager?

"To Ernesto's. I'm staying the night, so don't wait up. Not that you would."

He disappeared before she could light into him.

If he knew how many nights she did exactly that, watched and waited in the kitchen, wondering where he was...

She blinked back her tears of hurt and anger. Javier probably didn't even care how deeply his words had cut her, which made the burning in her eyes even worse.

She made her way numbly back to Benedict's truck. He came out as she approached and helped her in, then went back to the driver's seat.

"How was it?"

She stared at nothing for a time. "He... he won't go to college. Absolutely refuses."

How could she make Javier see how important this was? Why wouldn't he just listen to her?

"What will he do instead?"

She shrugged, then laughed humorlessly. "That's exactly what he did when I asked him that. Just shrugged, as if it didn't matter." Her voice rose on the last. "I don't know how to get through to him. I've tried and tried and tried and... nothing. And it's not the money—I've saved more than enough to send him wherever he might want to go."

All he had to do was show the slightest interest, exert the slightest effort, and he could go. She'd made it so easy for him.

"Where is he now?" Benedict asked. Gently, without reproach. It soothed away some of her hurt, the softness of Benedict's questioning.

"He—" She gestured wildly at the high school. "He said that he was crashing at a friend's, that I shouldn't wait up for him—not that I would anyway, is what he said."

She sniffed and bit at her wobbling lip. Okay, maybe the hurt wasn't really going away. Maybe it was getting worse.

Benedict handed her a tissue. "Teenagers are a pain in the ass."

She wiped at her eyes and tried to even out her breathing. She was so close to losing it; so, so close. "It's almost like he resents me. God, how badly did I screw up to make him act like this?"

"Hey." Benedict laid a hand on her shoulder and squeezed. "It's not you. This is normal for teenage boys. Even I was little shit when I was his age."

She gave him the side eye. "I really doubt that. You were probably born responsible."

He laughed. "I bet you were born that way too."

"No." She'd been a good student, a dutiful daughter before. It was only after she found herself responsible for Javier that she realized what true responsibility was. "I mean, I did all the good-girl things expected of me growing up. But when I got to college, I kind of pulled away from my family. I spent most weekends at school, didn't call that often. And I should have come home more, spent more time with all of them." She'd known at the time that it was the right thing to do, to go home whenever she could—and she hadn't. Which had made her parents' deaths hurt all the more.

"You didn't know what would happen." His thumb began to rub her shoulder, and that one little contact was so comforting. "College was your time, your achievement. You know how proud your parents were that you went. And now you want the same for Javier."

"Yeah, but he doesn't want it. And I don't know how to make him want it." She wiped her eyes once more, the tears slowing. But the hurt stayed, emptier now that she'd cried some of it out. "I'm sorry. You wasted over an hour on this."

"Wasn't a waste."

Kind of him to say so, but of course it was. He was Mr. Important Businessman—time was money and she'd just wasted both.

"I'll work late to make it up."

"It's almost five o'clock. I'd say we can quit early today." His hand left her shoulder and he turned the key in the ignition, the diesel roaring to life. "And I know just what'll make you feel better."

"What?" She stopped dabbing at her eyes to peer at him.

He grinned rather boyishly. "It's a surprise."

Benedict Merrill behaving like a schoolboy. She liked it. And she liked surprises. Maybe it would be a sexy one, involving the both of them getting buck naked. A distraction like that *would* make her feel better.

He turned them toward the resort but took them past the hotel and into the private area of the ranch, the part where only the family went. But they didn't take the road up to the family residences—instead, he took them down a dirt road that wound up into the hills. The truck climbed through vegetation made plump and green by spring rains, orange and yellow and purple splashes marking the patches of flowers. The buckwheat lining the road scraped at the truck as they passed, the narrowness of the track testifying to how little it was used.

Night crept on the higher they climbed so that, by the time he pulled off into a lookout, the sky was a deep purple going to black.

On the other side of the windshield, the ranch and resort were laid out on the valley floor below them. The pool was visible from here, a great glittering sapphire set amidst the pavé of the streetlights.

"Wow," she breathed. "It's so pretty." He was right; this was exactly what she'd needed, seeing Cabrillo shrunk down like this, sparkling amidst the mountains surrounding them. Her problems seemed much smaller from this perspective.

"Isn't it?" he asked, looking pleased that she was pleased.

"I bet you take all the girls here. Your own little private make-out spot." No one outside the family would likely have access to the road up.

"A few," he admitted. "Back in high school. I haven't been up here since senior year."

"Why not? It's gorgeous." Not that a man like him needed any help seducing a woman.

"Well, there was college," he said, "and then business school. When I came back, I started working at the ranch, and then Dad got sick and had to retire, and Josh..." He drummed his fingers on the steering wheel. "There just wasn't time."

For all that he was the son of the richest family in the area and she... wasn't, their time after college sounded very similar. Responsibility was the watchword of both their lives.

Only she was leaving in three months, her responsibility discharged. And he was staying for a lifetime of it. Rather sad to think of him all alone, trying to do the right thing by his family, the ranch, the resort, shouldering that burden for the rest of his life.

But he'd brought her here to be happy, not sad.

"Not even time to bring a woman up here to make out," she said with mock sympathy. "Pobrecito."

His gaze was hot, even in the dim light. "You're the first woman I've wanted to share this with."

God, that was romantic. Too romantic—she needed this to be only about sex so that she could leave in three months without leaving part of her heart behind.

She set a hand to his jaw and pulled him toward her, the stubble there deliciously raspy against her palm. It would be even more delicious along her inner thigh.

"Kiss me," she ordered softly.

He laughed gently, a caress of air against her lips. And then his mouth was on hers, as hungry as she was, as ready to devour as she was. She curled her fingers into his shirt and pulled, wanting more of him.

"Hang on," he gasped. He slid his seat all the way back, and in one quick, strong movement, he lifted her straight up onto his lap.

That was hot. So hot.

She leaned down to kiss him again, setting her hands on his shoulders for balance. The muscles there were as tense and hard as steel. His hands slid up her skirt, his thumbs hooking into her panties.

"Thank God you're not wearing those stupid tights," he muttered.

"I thought something like this might happen. Well, I *wanted* something like this to happen."

"The two of us necking like teenagers in the front seat of my truck?"

"Not this exactly. But now that it's happening, I wouldn't change any of it."

"I'd change the fact that I don't have any condoms on me." He smiled with tentative hope. "Do you have any?"

"Nope. Remembered to leave off my tights and forgot to pack the condoms."

He shook his head gravely, the twinkle in his eyes giving him away. "I ought to teach you a lesson. So that you don't forget again."

Her breasts tightened. "Really? What lesson might that be?"

"This." He swiped his fingers along her sex, through the fabric of her panties. A muted promise of what was to come when he breached that barrier.

"You're already so wet," he muttered into her neck. "Do you know how fucking hard that makes me, to feel that on my fingers?"

All she could give in response was a shaky moan.

He rubbed her clit, the fabric making it that much worse. She could feel the wetness now, her panties clinging to her folds.

And he'd only just started.

He nudged aside the cotton covering her, his fingers trailing along her inner thigh, catching in the ticklish fold that marked the boundary between her leg and her sex. She squirmed and moaned because he was so close and yet so far from where she wanted him, the tease.

"That's right, baby girl," he growled. "Tell me how much you like this. Moan for me. Scream for me."

How could she do anything but that now? "Make me scream," she dared him.

He set his thumb just above the head of her clit, heavy against the hood and the nerves buried there. Then he slid a forefinger inside her, slow and stretching—but not near as thick as his cock, which pressed hard and hot against her inner thigh...

He crooked his finger inside her even as his thumb made deliberate, deep circles around her clit—and she did it. She screamed as an orgasm tore her mind to shreds, her hips jerking out of her control, her lips sputtering out something like "Fuckfuckfuck."

She folded against him, burying her face into his shoulder as she tried to catch her breath and her thoughts.

That was quite possibly the best orgasm she'd ever had.

And they both had on all their clothes—although hers were askew—in the front seat of his truck.

And to think she could only cram in three months' worth of those orgasms.

"I won't forget the condoms next time," she promised solemnly.

He laughed, the force of it making her jiggle as he shook with it. "And I'll try to get us to a bed next time."

He kissed her on the corner of her mouth, a gentle touch that a man might give a woman he'd been giving orgasms to for forever.

But she wouldn't be that woman. This was only for three months.

"What about you?" she asked, wanting to put this back into safe—and solely physical—territory.

"Me?"

"Well…" She slipped the tongue of his belt free of the buckle, the one he'd been wearing forever, the one she remembered him holding in that newspaper photo. "I figure you had just as much of a responsibility as me to bring the condoms. So maybe I should make sure you don't forget."

His smile came on as slowly as his hands slid up her ass. "Yeah, you probably should."

She leaned back until she was lying against the steering wheel. His eyelids were heavy, and he sprawled as if he hadn't a care in the world—but his fingers sank tight into the curve of her ass, and his cock pushed hard against the zipper of his jeans.

"That looks painful," she said with mock innocence. She rubbed his bulge, loving the choked moan he made. "Better?"

He only lifted his hips to rub himself against her hand again.

"Hmm, maybe not. Let's take a closer look." She flicked his jeans button open, then slowly, slowly, lowered the zipper.

He bit his lower lip, the lines of his neck going stark. She leaned in, took his lower lip gently between her own teeth, and tugged it free, sucking on it for a moment.

And then she pulled out his cock. She couldn't see it in any great detail, but it felt long, the skin smooth, the head softer, with a slippery bead of moisture at the tip. She wrapped her fingers around it and slid down and up and back again until her hand was buried in the nest of hair there.

But she could make this a lot better for him. She lifted her hand to her mouth and ran her tongue over her palm.

"Jesus," he wheezed. "Do that again."

She widened her eyes. "This?" And she did it slow and nasty that time, watching his reaction. His eyes went wide, then fluttered to half mast. Such a delicious expression on him.

She grabbed his cock again and started to pump, her hand slick with spit and his own fluid. He lifted his hips with each stroke, trying to drive himself deeper into her hand. He bared his teeth, gripped her ass as if she were the only thing holding him to the earth, and grunted.

"That's right, baby," she crooned. "Tell me how much you like it."

"So fucking much," he ground out. He rolled his hips, lifting both of them clear off the seat. "The door... tissues..." He reached for them, only to jerk his hips helplessly once more.

She grabbed them instead, just in time to catch his come. He released a low, tortured sound as his cock spasmed with his release.

"Jesus," he said, dazed. "Jesus Christ."

She'd never seen him so disheveled, so knocked for a loop. Even in all her dirty imaginings, he'd always been cool, in control. She was the one screaming and losing her head.

Which she'd definitely done here, but to make him look like he did now, all inside out and pleasure wrecked? It was heady stuff.

"Tissues," she said, with an amused shake of her head. Any other man would have simply thought, "Damn these clothes—I'm about to come."

"I couldn't come into your hand," he said, embarrassment shading the words.

Now it was her turn to put a soft kiss on his lips. He was so chivalrous, even when she was giving him a hand job in a make-out spot in his truck. It was really cute.

His expression went solemn, and he smoothed her hair from her face, leaving his hand to cup her cheek. And then he just stared, as if he couldn't look at her enough. He leaned in, kissed the corner of her mouth again.

"Thank you, baby," he whispered, serious as a heart attack. "Thank you."

Suddenly she wanted to cry. She ought to say it was nothing, but right now... right now it felt like everything.

Chapter 5

THE RAP AT HER FRONT door had Pilar cursing—although it was a Sunday and she tried very hard not to take the Lord's name in vain on that day.

But she had one leg in her tights and one not, and now she'd have to wriggle into the other leg as quickly as she could before whoever was there left because taking off the tights would take just as long as putting them on.

"Coming," she yelled, hopping on one foot to the door and pulling on the tights as she did.

There. One last shimmy and tug and she was ready.

Except for her skirt.

"Fu—crap," she muttered. "Be right there," she called again.

A dash back to her room, grabbing the doorknob to keep from falling as she put on her skirt, and then a dash back to the entryway.

Whoever had knocked had better still be there.

She opened the door to find Lucia, her neighbor, holding a bulging black trash bag.

"She gave you more?" Pilar asked. "How much shopping does that woman do?"

Lucia shrugged. "She has the money for it. Can you take them to the consignment shop for me?"

Pilar took the bag, her arm dropping at the weight of it. "Are you sure there's nothing in there you want?"

Lucia gave a quick laugh. "No, she hasn't shrunk to my height yet. But you take whatever you want."

"I doubt she's filled out to my size either," Pilar answered.

The two of them eyed the bag and began to laugh together. Lucia's employer meant well, giving Lucia her gently used designer clothes, but Mrs. Detlan could best be described as X-ray thin and giraffe tall—which Lucia wasn't. And neither was Pilar.

But the money from the consignment store was always welcome to Lucia, and someone else—closer in size to Mrs. Detlan—got to enjoy new clothes.

"I'll take them in tomorrow," Pilar promised. Lucia's English was good, but her accent made her difficult to understand unless you'd known her awhile. "Oh, and I have that novela recorded for you on DVD."

"Oh! Did you watch the latest one? What happened with Rodrigo?"

"No." Pilar made a face. "I haven't liked it as much since they killed off Manuel. Rodrigo just isn't the same."

"But he isn't really dead..." Lucia trailed off as she turned to look down the street.

The low grumble of a diesel reverberated through the neighborhood. Hugo had a diesel, but it didn't sound quite like that one—

Oh no. Pilar knew that truck. She'd had a screaming

orgasm in it just three days ago. *Please don't stop, just be driving through...*

The truck parked right in front of her house.

What the hell was he doing coming here?

They were supposed to be discreet about whatever it was that they were doing. And she had to be at Mass in half an hour.

Benedict climbed out. He was wearing a light blue button-down, black jeans, and a black Stetson pulled low over his eyes. He looked... ready for church. Or maybe he was coming from church. Maybe he was one of those annoying people who went to the early Mass because it was quieter and more formal.

"Pilar." He touched his hat as he came up the walk. "Lucia."

Ooooh, touching his hat like that, like an old-timey cowboy paying his respect to a lady... She blew out a breath, wriggled her toes in her tights. He melted her with that stuff.

Lucia gave her a quick look that said *What is this?*

Pilar's answering look said, *I don't know.* She certainly couldn't explain the appearance of the Merrill heir on her front steps on a Sunday morning.

Now if it had been a Saturday night...

"I've got to get ready for church," Lucia said with a wave. "I'll see you later."

Traitor. But Lucia didn't hear the insult Pilar thought at her and beat her retreat.

She faced down her boss, shoeless and holding a bag of charity clothes. "Did I forget something at work?" she chirped.

"No." He took off his hat, tapped it against his thigh. It

hadn't even mussed his hair. How did he do that? "I thought I might take you to church."

To church? That wasn't discreet or private—that was *dating*.

"I go to the Spanish Mass," she said.

"I know. I speak Spanish."

"You speak Castilian," she countered.

"Huh. I didn't know the Spanish translation was so different from the English." He grinned at her.

Beast. Of course he'd be able to follow along—she'd only wanted to give him an out. And he wasn't taking it.

She wanted to cross her arms and glare at him, but she was still holding the trash bag. "I thought this was supposed to be a secret."

He sighed. "Maybe this was a bad idea. But... I really wanted to see you."

Jesus. Did he intend for her insides to liquefy when he said that? "I... I missed you too."

It was true. She'd spent yesterday wondering what he was up to. Did he spend his weekends working? What did he do for fun? He must have fun sometime. He laughed too much not to.

He ran a hand through his hair, pushing back that unruly bit she loved, and gave her an intent look. "If you don't want me to take you, I won't," he said. "But I really, really want to."

Walking into Mass with Benedict Merrill was going to be a whole new level of notoriety. If they weren't swarmed at the end of the service by curious parishioners, she'd eat this bag of clothes.

But she was leaving in three months. Of course, she'd come back to visit, but she wouldn't have to live every day with the gossip. And why not leave in a blaze of glory? Or at least the minor blaze that attending church with Benedict would ignite.

"Sure, why not?" she asked.

Wait, had she just used the exact same words as when she'd said yes to this affair business? What was it about this solid, responsible man that made her so reckless?

That smile he was giving her right now, the one she hadn't even known existed before agreeing to his crazy, sexy scheme—that smile was probably the reason.

"We can get some menudo at Pancho's after if you want."

He knew the way to her heart. "If you're buying, I'm eating."

He looked toward the front door questioningly. Oh Lord, she'd have to invite him inside, and the place was... Well, she hadn't been expecting company. Maybe he'd wait here while she got her shoes?

"Is Javier coming?"

Crap. She'd rather he'd asked to see the house. "He refuses to come to church," she answered stiffly. That had been a battle royale, one she'd lost. "But he came home last night."

Little victories. She had to savor the little victories.

"Well, it'll just be the two of us then." He held out his arm for her.

So chivalrous. A girl could get used to this attention. And the look in his eyes, as if she'd made him so happy. And proud. It looked a lot like... like *love.*

And that didn't completely scare her.

She stepped toward him, meaning to take his arm and—

"Crap." A pebble on the walkway cut hard into her heel, right through her tights. "Can you wait here while I get my shoes?"

PILAR COULD CONFIDENTLY SAY she now knew how rock stars felt—if they were the kind of rock stars who went to church.

Every eye was on them as they walked down the aisle. She picked a likely looking pew—near the middle, kind of empty—made her reverence, and sat down.

Benedict acted as if he didn't notice at all, coming to sit next to her with easy assurance, as if he always attended this service, as if no one—instead of everyone—was staring at them.

Her parents' friends peered with suspicious gazes. Little Pilar Lopez coming in with Benedict Merrill was not good. They were worried for her.

But her friends... her friends stared just as hard, but with a winking twist that said, *Benedict Merrill? How'd you do that?*

He asked me to have an affair. And I said, Sure, why not?

She coughed into her hand to keep from laughing out loud. Laughter was certain to make the older generation that much sniffier about the entire situation.

Benedict leaned in, not lasciviously, but almost husbandlike. It gave her hot chills all over, the way he bent himself toward her.

"All right?" he asked softly.

"Yeah."

She tried to keep her attention on the service, but it was difficult with him next to her and everyone's covert attention on them. For his part, Benedict went through the Mass with an expression of attentive serenity. Some of the nosier ladies could take lessons from him on maintaining a properly reflective demeanor.

After the service ended, they were mobbed as she'd predicted. But not just by curiosity seekers; several prominent people stopped to talk to him about projects he was involved with in the community. Standing next to him, making small talk with the spouses as Benedict went about being… well, *Benedict,* she felt rather First Ladyish.

And she liked it. Which she shouldn't have, considering she wanted to be free of the Merrill family and not dating one of its members.

Later, they were tucking into steaming bowls of menudo at Pancho's, the place surprisingly slow for a Sunday morning.

"Does everyone stare at you like that every Sunday?" he asked casually.

"Pfft. Everyone was staring at you and you know it."

The bells on the door jangled as a couple came in. The man spotted them and called out, "Benedict! How are you today?"

Benedict nodded and said, "Pretty good. And yourself?"

"Can't complain."

They went up to order and Pilar leaned in toward Benedict and whispered, "You're always on, aren't you?"

His jaw twitched as his expression went wary. "What do you mean?"

"I mean whenever you're out in public, you have to be *Benedict Merrill.* Everyone in this town knows you or your family. Everyone expects you to be this—this community leader, successful businessman, glad-hander all the time." The easy, funny Benedict he was with her when they were alone—that wasn't the Benedict the rest of Cabrillo got.

He swirled his spoon through his bowl, studying it grimly. "I'm not complaining about it," he muttered. "I know I'm lucky to have the life I do."

"I never said you were complaining." She didn't think she'd ever heard him complain, not once. "Just that it must be exhausting."

He smiled, all wry self-deprecation. "I'm not a rock star or anything. Once I leave Cabrillo, no one gives a damn who I am."

She'd care. No matter where he went.

Which meant that when she left Cabrillo, she might not leave her feelings for him behind. They might be too deep to easily shake off.

Crap.

She took a sip of coffee, trying to corral her thoughts. And her silly feelings.

"Well, I guess you're used to it," she said, "being stared at like that."

"Me? Why would they stare at me?" He gave her a lazy perusal. "Now you—who wouldn't want to stare at you?"

Heat bloomed on her skin. "I thought we were going to be discreet. Secret lovers."

"I was discreet. You wouldn't believe the things I was imagining during Mass—and I never did one."

She couldn't help but laugh. "And here I was thinking that you were just being pious."

His gaze went hot. "I'm good at looking innocent. In fact, I'm imagining all kinds of things—things involving you naked—right now."

She dropped her voice. "You can't ravish me in Pancho's. The menudo's too good—I want to be able to come back here again."

His laugh was addictive. The more he did it, the more she wanted to make him do it.

"God, I really did miss you," he said.

Missed her? But he saw her all week. Of course, she'd missed him too...

"What did you do yesterday?" she asked. "Did you work?"

"Most Saturdays I do," he admitted. "But I had a lot of thinking to do yesterday, so I went for a long ride through the preserve." Before she could ask him what he'd had to think about, he went on: "What did you do yesterday?"

"Chores. Painted my nails. Read." A boring Saturday. Which were sometimes the nicest kind.

"Your e-reader working out well then?"

It had been a Christmas gift from him two years ago. At first she'd thought it was impersonal—that everyone who worked for him got one. But when he'd asked her if she liked it and what she was reading on it, she realized he'd bought it just for her. Because he knew she liked to read.

She'd never explicitly told him that, but he'd known.

"I love it," she told him. "But I think you already know that."

The moment between them slowed, stretched.

"I do," he said carefully.

"And you know I eat peanut butter sandwiches every day."

He pulled his spoon through his bowl, his gaze never leaving hers. "I do."

"What else have you noticed about me?"

He dropped his spoon, his gaze taking on weight. "We've worked side by side for five years. I couldn't help but"—an odd catch there, as if he meant to say something different —"couldn't help but notice things. You probably noticed stuff about me too."

If someone had asked her a week ago what she'd noticed about Benedict, she'd have given some quip about his ass in

Wranglers. But she would have been using that flippancy as a shield, to deflect from the truth she was only just now beginning to understand.

She'd noticed that he was decent, and responsible, and thoughtful. Not really nice, at least not how most people used the word, but... compassionate. Considerate.

On some level, she'd known that before. He had, after all, given her the job. But seeing this new, easier side to him made her understanding of him go beyond the superficial.

And her attraction to him went beyond that as well.

She swallowed hard and tried to come up with something light, amusing. You didn't tell a man that kind of stuff over menudo in Pancho's.

"You like to read too," she said finally. "But only nonfiction. And thrillers. You like those."

He went still, attentive. As if deeply curious to know what she knew about him. "Yeah. What else?"

"You like baked salmon with garlic mashed potatoes for lunch."

A smile twitched at his mouth. "Well, it beats peanut butter sandwiches. Go on."

Food and books: stuff that almost everyone liked. She wanted to give him something more personal.

"You're very focused," she began. "You work hard, not to build wealth for yourself but for your family. To preserve what was passed on to you so you can pass it on to those coming after. You feel responsible for everyone around you—and feel it deeply when you can't protect them all."

Maybe that was too personal. But it beat *I might be falling in love with the way you care for me.*

He stared at her, food forgotten, his gaze starkly open. "Are you talking about me?" he asked slowly. "Or yourself?"

Whoops. When she'd wanted to make her answer more personal, she hadn't meant to get so... *personal.*

"Maybe both of us," she admitted shakily. "But this is much too philosophical for a Sunday morning."

"What better day to get philosophical than on a Sunday?" His gaze was too intent, too piercing—it made her feel exposed. Unnerved.

"Not this Sunday." Cheery and light as she tried to get away from this heavy mood between them. "I have to go repair sink pipes—can't be too philosophical then."

"Your sink is leaking?" The way his mouth set made her heart drop. She hadn't been fishing for help.

"I'm not asking you to fix it," she said. "I can handle it myself." Oh, much too rude and snappy, but wasn't the whole point of this to stop having Benedict do things for her? It didn't help that in her heart of hearts, she wanted him to fix the sink. Mucking about down there was not her idea of a good time.

It didn't matter how much she liked having him fix stuff for her—falling in love with him because he took care of her would be the worst mistake of her life.

"I know you can handle it yourself," he said quietly. As if she'd hurt his feelings. "But I want to do it for you."

And now she felt all bitchy. He didn't know she was tied up in knots about continually taking his charity. He thought they were just having an affair—he probably fixed all his girlfriends' sinks. He was that kind of guy.

"Sorry, I didn't mean to snap at you," she said. "If you really want to take a look, you're welcome to."

An hour later he was under her sink, doing something pretty strenuous with a wrench, while a fearsome smell came from the disconnected pipes.

"I guess I should have cleaned out the pipes before you

did this," she said weakly, holding her hand over her nose. He was going to ruin that shirt of his. And the smell was probably getting into his hair.

"No worries," he called from under the sink. "We'll just pour a shit ton of drain cleaner down it when I'm done."

She propped her hip against the kitchen counter and watched him work. Or watched his legs, really, since the rest of him was under the sink. Having a man fix something for her was pretty nice.

Having Benedict Merrill fix something for her was better than nice. He was lean hipped, flat stomached—and the way he cocked one leg was kind of hot. Which was kind of silly, because all he was doing was bending his knee, but it did things to her to see him like that in her kitchen. Relaxed enough to get underneath her sink and cock his leg as he worked.

Her parents had spent countless Sundays just like this, her dad fixing something around the house while her mom watched and gave advice.

Pilar slid her hand along the counter, her fingers finding the note Javier had left.

Gone to Hugo's—won't be back till tomorrow.

Never asked if he could, never told her what he might be doing at Hugo's—she might have been his roommate for all the consideration he'd shown her.

But at least he'd left a note.

Don't let him get into trouble, she prayed. *Please give him the sense to stay out of trouble.*

Benedict swore at something from under the sink, and a wave of stench came from the drain. Poor guy, stuck fixing her sink and getting coated with stinky gunk on a Sunday.

She sighed. Real life was so very unsexy. If only she lived

in a romance novel—then they'd be banging on the kitchen counters by this point.

"What time is it?" he called from under the sink.

"About three," she answered. He had to be home in time for Sunday dinner—the entire Merrill family gathered for dinner on Sunday nights and had for as long as she could remember.

She wasn't a Merrill, so she'd eat some frozen entree from a cardboard tray here at home.

His hand came out from the cabinet and felt around the floor.

"Do you need something?" she asked. Finally, she could be a little helpful.

His amazing stomach tightened as he lifted up to look out. "That pipe." He pointed.

She handed it to him, and he went back to wrestling with the pipes, grunting with whatever he was doing.

"Got it," he announced triumphantly. "Or at least, I think I do. Run the water."

She flipped on the faucet, bracing herself for his shouts of outrage if the pipes leaked.

"Okay, turn it off," he said after a few moments. He slid out from the cabinet, his hair falling over his forehead, his sleeves rolled up to his elbows, and grease streaked across his shirt. At least, she hoped it was grease and not black sink muck.

"I can try to wash your shirt," she offered hesitantly. But she might not be able to save it. How much were his shirts? She supposed he could take that out of her salary along with the tires.

He looked down at himself, then climbed to his feet. "Don't worry about it."

"At least let me get you one of Javier's shirts. You don't

want to rub that all over your truck seats. Will you have time to shower before dinner?"

His smile went wicked. "Why? Gonna offer to let me use yours?"

Yes. And can I share it with you? "You're, uh, welcome to..." *Stop blushing.* "I'll just grab one of Javier's shirts for you."

She went to slip away, but he set a hand on the counter, blocking her in. She swallowed hard as all of her went tingly and tense. She slowly lifted her face to his.

He looked like he could eat her up in one snap of his jaws, then lick his chops after.

"If I didn't have this dinner to go to..."

Yes. This was what should be between them, this pressing heat, this smoldering awareness. Not all that caring romance stuff.

"What would you do?" she breathed.

He stepped closer, forcing her against the counter, her back bowing as she made space for him where she'd been. "I'd have you bent over in that shower," he growled, "water pouring down the both of us as you gripped the bar, me fucking you from behind. It'd be so good, baby. So hard, but so good."

She made a noise of want, of need, of pure feral greed. *Oh yes, let's go do that.*

"I know." He stepped away. "I know. But we can't today. Now go get that shirt before I lose it and get grease all over your clothes when I tear them off."

If he thought she could walk after that little speech... But her legs held when she peeled herself away from the counter and wobbled off to Javier's room.

When she came back, he'd put all the tools away and was washing his hands.

"I got it." She held out the shirt to him. He finished drying his hands, took the shirt and stripped off his own.

She sucked in a breath. His stomach wasn't just flat—it was *etched*. She could spend the rest of her life exploring the peaks and valleys of those abs.

He wore a half smile when her gaze returned to his face. He knew exactly how hot he was. How hot she found him.

"Before I go..." He pulled her close to him, kissed her on the corner of her mouth. "We have time for a few things."

She hoped *a few things* wouldn't leave her a sloppy mess of unfulfilled lust.

He flicked open the first button of her shirt. "Mind if I take yours off too?"

"You already are," she pointed out.

"If you say no," he reminded her, "I'll listen."

"And if I say yes?"

"I'll listen then too."

"Then... yes."

He took his time unbuttoning her—more to tease her she knew, since the bastard had a little smirk playing at his lips the entire time. He meant to torment her by being so damn slow. Well, she could play cool too.

She waited for his reaction to her bra. It was black and lacy and decently sexy—but still, she couldn't contain the girls in anything like a cute little demi cup.

His response once her shirt was off didn't disappoint. His lips parted, and his intake of breath was perilously close to a gasp.

"Oh, Pilar." He cupped her in his hands, taking another sharp breath. Just as she'd imagined, his hands fit her perfectly. "You've got such fantastic tits. Better than I even imagined."

"They're kind of big." They were more than *kind of big*—

they'd been such an embarrassment when they'd sprung up when she was fifteen.

He scowled ferociously. "Can tits ever be too big?"

She giggled, then gasped as his thumbs found her nipples and flicked. "But they are big. Just like my ass and my belly—"

He kissed her, hard, stealing those words before she could finish. "I love all of it. Every inch. I love all of you."

Oh, that was dangerously close to *I love you*. Which he didn't.

Did he?

He couldn't. No way.

He flicked open the front closure of the bra, spilling her breasts into his waiting hands. And she couldn't remember to be worried, not when he was stroking and kneading so perfectly. He found her nipple with his thumb and forefinger and squeezed.

She gasped.

"Too hard?" he whispered.

She shook her head. "It... no, it's good."

"How about this?" He lowered his head and took her nipple between his teeth—not hard enough to really hurt, just enough to let her know they were sharp.

It was exactly how she liked it, the pleasure rising faster than it ever had before. She held his head as she urged him on with her moans, the roll of her hips.

"I bet I could make you come like this," he said, all harsh heat. "Have you ever done that?"

He took the peak in his mouth again, flicking with his tongue, and holy Jesus—what had he been asking?

"No one's ever tried," she managed to get out, a pant coming with every word.

He made a tutting noise. "Stick with me, babe, and I'll do you right."

Oh, he would too. He'd do her right into another of the best orgasms of her life.

"Please, yes, let's try," she begged. If he would put his mouth back where it had been, and maybe his hand between her legs—that would do her very nicely.

"I'll do anything you want," he promised, "for as long as you want—"

Briippp. His phone squawked from his pocket, shattering the moment.

"Fuck," he muttered. Exactly what she wanted to say. He glanced behind him at the microwave clock. "I'm late. And that's probably Liliana."

Family called. So Benedict would go.

That wasn't entirely fair—the family Sunday dinner was a tradition. Her time today with him was a bonus. Not an obligation.

She picked up the shirt, shoved it at him. "You'd better go. If you don't want to be any later."

He ignored the shirt in her hand, his hands going to her bra. He gently tucked her back into it, then buttoned up her shirt. When he was done, he set his hands along her jaw. "This isn't finished."

She was beginning to suspect that this wouldn't be finished even after she left. But she wanted him. She was almost shaking with it, so badly did she want to complete what they'd started.

"Of course not," she answered, wrapping her arms around herself to try to damp the flames he'd ignited. His phone squawked again. "But we both have family obligations."

He rubbed his thumb along her jaw, studying her with

those deep blue eyes. Maybe he was thinking of staying, of calling off the family dinner...

"Damn," he muttered. He put a kiss at the corner of her mouth. "I'll see you tomorrow."

No, he wasn't staying. And truthfully, she didn't want him to blow off his family. His commitment to them was one of the best things about him.

He tugged on Javier's shirt—*good-bye, delicious abs, until we meet again*—and was out the door.

She crumpled up her brother's note and tossed it into the trash. No need to feel sorry for herself for spending a Sunday evening alone. In fact, it was the perfect opportunity to research cities to move to in three months.

The idea wasn't as exciting as it had been before she'd handed Benedict her resignation.

Chapter 6

WHEN BENEDICT WALKED INTO THE office the next morning, Pilar did not get the reception she'd been expecting.

"Morning," she chirped as Benedict strode past her to his office door, looking lean hipped and long legged in his usual jeans, his hair beginning to slip over his forehead.

She pulled her shoulders back and sucked her belly in, the better for him to see the new blouse she was wearing. Her breasts looked spectacular in it, if she did say so herself. Spectacular, but still professional. And yesterday he'd proved that he liked her tits. *Really* liked them.

"Morning," he muttered, giving her a spare glance before disappearing behind his office door.

Her spine slumped. Well... well, that had sucked. He'd never before been so curt. He always asked how she was, how things were going, what was on the agenda for the day, no matter how busy he was.

And they were supposed to be having an affair.

She was still his admin though. Time to go be his admin.

She marched into his office, finding him standing

behind his desk, knuckles braced against it as he peered at his computer.

"Your schedule for today has been updated," she told him.

His gaze flicked to her for half a moment, then flicked back to the screen. "I know."

That was rather short. And chilled.

"Is there anything you'd like to go over this morning?" Brisk, efficient, professional. Which was how they were supposed to be on company time.

"No." He glanced at the door. "That's all."

Okay. She could handle this, although it hurt a little, especially after he'd felt her up in her kitchen yesterday. And taken her to church. But she wanted this distance between them at work.

Only—not quite so distant. Not quite so cold.

"Call me if you need anything."

He didn't look up.

So she left.

He remained short-tempered throughout the morning, answering her every request with monosyllables, his gaze sliding off her each time he glanced her way. By noon she felt small and stupid and smashed.

The affair had been his idea, but maybe he'd changed his mind. He could have told her that rather than engage in this cold-shoulder business. She could take a hint—she wouldn't cling to him when she wasn't wanted.

She smashed her fist into the stapler much harder than necessary, enjoying the sharp metallic crunch as the staple bit through the stack of papers.

Thank God she was leaving in three months. She never would have imagined Benedict could transform into an asshole so quickly, but better to know now.

At noon, she poked her head into his office, not willing to come any closer and face his bruising avoidance. "Anything else before I leave for lunch?"

She wasn't leaving, only slinking off to find a hidden corner to eat her peanut butter sandwich, but he didn't need to know that. Let him think she had a hot lunch date.

He glanced up from his paperwork and looked at her—really *looked* at her—for the first time that day. His expression was stark, his eyes haunted—he was... *anguished*.

What had happened?

She crossed his office in a flash. "Are you okay?"

She wanted to clasp his arm, his hand, anything to ease that expression on his face. But the desk was between them.

"Could you have lunch with me?" The harshness of his words almost disguised the pleading in his tone. "Somewhere not here. I have to talk to you."

Her stomach wrung itself out. "Uh... look I can take a hint. You don't have to do this." *Steady. Don't break down in his office.* "In fact, I'd rather not even talk about it. Clean break and all that."

But it didn't feel clean. It felt ragged and bleeding.

He frowned at her. "What—" His voice dropped. "You think I want to end this?"

What else was she supposed to think, what with him acting like an iceberg and then announcing, *We have to talk?*

"Well, you've been very distant today," she said. "I thought..."

But Benedict wouldn't do that. He wasn't a callow high schooler. He'd never end things like that—he'd be direct, honest, open. So why was he acting like this?

Something must have happened. And she was the one acting like a teenager, assuming it was all about their relationship.

"No," he rasped, "I don't want to end this. I just... I need to talk to you. But not about us."

Us. It was only supposed to be sex, short-lived, flaring like a struck match, and burning out just as quickly. But when he said *us*, she found herself aching for something more. Something longer. Something permanent.

You're leaving in three months. Starting a new life in three months. You can't be Benedict Merrill's charity case for the rest of your life.

But she could be his comfort in this moment.

"Sure," she answered. "Let me grab my purse."

They drove in silence to the café down the road. She had to admit having someone drive her around was such a comforting luxury. After her parents' accident, driving had made her terrified. But she kept at it until getting behind the wheel inspired only dull panic.

Being chauffeured by Benedict was the closest she came to being unfazed by driving in forever.

Benedict pulled the truck into a spot in the café parking lot, killed the engine... and stared at the dashboard.

"How are your new tires?" he asked dully.

Tires? "They're good. New, you know."

He nodded slowly, never cracking a smile. "Good. I'm glad. I'm glad to know you're safe, that you're driving something safe." His fingers wrapped around the wheel and went tight, as if he needed something to cling to.

She'd never seen him so rattled. It touched a deep part of her, a part that she should not allow him access to. But it was too late.

"You wanted to talk about my tires then?" She knew he didn't, but it seemed like he needed a push to get to his real point.

His fingers eased on the wheel. "No." He let go. "Josh wants me to come see him."

So that was it. She pulled a breath through her teeth. "Are you going to go?"

"I have to."

She closed her eyes for half a moment. Of course that was what Benedict would say. Not *I don't know* or *I don't want to*—there was never any question he'd honor Josh's request. And nothing about how he felt about it.

But he was obviously upset. And so invested in his role as the unfeeling, rock-solid head of both the family and the business he couldn't even discuss it with her in the office.

"What do you think he wants to talk about?" she asked, keeping her voice neutral. Neither Benedict nor Josh needed judgment from her right now.

Benedict sighed deeply. "Before he left, I told him—I told him that he needed to go to jail." His hands clenched around the wheel again. "That he needed to be punished for what he'd done. That I prayed the experience would be a true reformation for him."

She tried to imagine saying such things to Javier should he be sent to prison. Imagined Javier's reaction to that. Her heart wanted to shrink to nothing at just the thought.

How terrible for Benedict and his brother.

"He probably didn't take that very well."

He gave a humorless laugh. "No. He said he didn't want to see me again."

The hurt in his voice sliced at her.

"But you still tried to visit him, didn't you?" She didn't know why she asked when she already knew the answer.

"Of course," he answered. "He's my little brother. He might have deserved it, but I still worry about him in that place. He never let me see him though."

She watched his hands on the wheel, clenching and unclenching with the emotion he only barely allowed to creep into his voice. "When are you going?" she asked gently.

"Saturday." And then the emotions broke free, twisting in his words. "I don't know, Pilar. If he's still not ready to grow up, if *prison* hasn't turned him around... what will?" He took a shuddering breath and another and another.

She slid her hands over his, pried them free of the steering wheel, and held them. Large hands, the hands of a man who carried a lot of responsibility. "I can't tell you that everything will be all right," she said. "I can't tell you what to do to make it better." She wished she could though. "All I can tell you is that you're doing your best. You're a good man. And a good brother."

She kissed the corner of his mouth, just as he always did to her. As her lips met that spot—gently firm lips, raspy stubble, and the subtle upquirk he always wore—she understood why he liked to kiss her there. It was somehow more intimate than a regular kiss—anyone might claim a person's mouth, but who would think to point to the corner and say that, that little patch is mine?

Only someone who knew every inch of that mouth already.

She rubbed his knuckles, wanting to soothe him. He bent his head as his fingers curled around hers and held tightly. "I knew talking to you would make me feel better," he said. Softer, easier than before. "I knew you would understand."

Of course she understood. He carried so many burdens —the running of the ranch and the resort and worrying about his siblings and cousins and parents—and he did it unflinchingly.

But who ever helped him? She knew Liliana went to visit Josh too—but did Liliana impress upon their brother the necessity of changing his ways? Did Liliana ever speak hard truths to Josh?

Likely not. They all left it up to Benedict, no doubt. And Josh had turned on him for it.

"Is anyone going with you?" she asked. Because if no one else was, she damn well would.

"Liliana and my parents."

That hurt. Hurt that she couldn't claim a spot next to him, to help support him. But she was only his assistant. She'd asked to keep their relationship secret.

"That's great," she said unconvincingly. "They'll be there for you then."

He studied her for long moments, the intensity of his gaze making her want to squirm. It wasn't sexual or sad—it was intimate in a way she'd never before seen from a man. And never before seen in Benedict.

She wanted to hide from that gaze, to tell him she wasn't ready yet—but not ready for what? She didn't know.

"Come to dinner on Sunday," he finally said.

Oh boy. She wanted to. Wanted to watch him among his family. Wanted to see how relaxed and happy he probably was with them, away from the business. But—

She shook her head. "That's probably not such a good idea. People might suspect."

He pulled her hand closer to him and laid it across his chest. She could feel the beat of his heart—steady, even.

More romance. Harder and harder to resist with every gesture he gave her.

"Liliana loves you," he said, "and so does everyone else. You're a friend of the family. Bring Javier too."

"Huh. If he decides to show up on Sunday."

He brought her knuckles to his lips and kissed them. Because he understood her too. She released a breath. "Okay. Dinner on Sunday it is. And if I can corral Javier, he'll be there too."

Benedict's smile was filled with delight—and relief. He really did want her to come.

But of course he did. Benedict didn't play games. He was true and honest and direct, an honorable man trying to do what was best for his family. Even if what he had to do hurt him.

Just like she was trying to do with Javier.

A surge of sympathy, of understanding, knocked straight into her heart, tumbling it end over end. She might want to keep their relationship quiet, might want to pretend it was only a physical thing between them, but it wasn't.

She might just be falling for him.

A MERRILL SUNDAY dinner was a boisterous affair. Not because of Benedict—he was always the quiet one in any large gathering—but because of his two siblings and their cousin.

They were all gathered at the main house, the one that Liliana and Luke shared now that their parents had retired to the Central Coast.

Pilar was laughing at a shaggy-dog story Liliana and Luke were spinning about their recent trip to Vegas, her sides aching as she tried to catch her breath. Liliana and Luke kept trying to one-up each other with witty remarks and snarky asides.

Their cousin, Penny Moreno, was laughing just as hard, along with her boyfriend. The boyfriend was new, at least to

Pilar. Apparently he and Penny had dated for years, broken up several months ago, then gotten back together when he was injured on the bull-riding circuit. Judging by how googly-eyed they were, she'd never guess they'd ever broken up.

Benedict watched it all with a small smile on his face, happy to observe from the sidelines.

She wanted to go sit next to him, to tease him until he started laughing as unreservedly as the rest of them. But he looked content enough, and it would seem odd. They weren't friends—Liliana and Penny were her friends.

Liliana and Luke finished their story with a flourish, Luke going over to talk with Penny's boyfriend when the laughter died down.

Liliana sidled up next to Pilar, a beer clutched in her hand. "Javier couldn't come?"

She'd never actually seen her brother today to ask if he could. "No, he's busy with schoolwork."

"Has he registered for classes yet?" Easy for Liliana to assume that everyone would do as she had and just slide into college right from high school.

"No, not yet," she said. "But there's still time."

There wasn't.

"Not much," Liliana said, frowning.

And what the hell am I supposed to do about it? But she couldn't yell at Liliana—the other woman was only trying to make small talk. And Pilar couldn't hog-tie Javier and force him to go to college.

She only wished things could be that easy.

"It's his decision." And soon, she'd have to find a way to let go of that responsibility for Javier. But hopefully she could convince him to enroll before she had to do that.

She flicked a glance toward Benedict, who was still

watching everyone. When had he let go of Josh? Or had he ever? Was responsibility—failed responsibility—even now gnawing at his gut?

Judging by his reaction to Josh's request to see him, it definitely was. There had been only fleeting opportunities for a private moment with Benedict this past week, thanks to an unusually busy schedule for him. And she hadn't had a chance today to ask how yesterday's visit had gone.

His posture was relaxed, his smile unstrained—but he was holding himself apart from everyone.

"How did Benedict take the news that you're leaving?" Liliana asked in an arch tone.

Pilar gave Liliana a sharp look, but the other girl only took a swig of her beer. "Fine. He's upset that he'll have to get used to a new assistant, but he'll adjust."

Liliana laughed, disbelief coloring her mirth. "I'll just bet he took it fine."

"Why would you say that?" Did Liliana suspect something was going on?

"Because he's been crazy about you from the start." Blunt and direct.

"What?" *No.* No, Liliana was wrong. It was only an affair between them. Any crazy, inconvenient emotions were all on Pilar's side.

"Come on. All we hear is *Pilar did this, Pilar did that, Pilar and I worked on this, Pilar and I worked on that.* He never talks about work off the clock unless you're somehow involved."

"But... he's my boss. He's never"—*at least not before* —"never done anything to suggest..."

To suggest that he had deeper feelings for her. It had all been cool efficiency from him.

Until she'd given him her resignation.

"Of course he wouldn't," Liliana said. "Benedict suffers

in silence. And you've got Javier—he wouldn't want to make things complicated for you. I always thought that once Javier was on his own…"

"Thought what?"

"That Benedict would make his move."

Well, the other girl was wrong about that. Benedict had made his move before. And crazy about her? No, that couldn't be right. He only talked about her because they spent all day together.

She looked over at him, only to catch him staring at her. When their eyes met, his lips tipped in a small, secret smile. One that spoke of intimate secrets, of moments shared only between the two of them. The kind of smile that held volumes.

Shit. He *was* crazy about her. And he'd hidden it all this time.

When he'd said that he'd been attracted to her from the very beginning… Her cheeks heated as his words took on new meaning.

He's been crazy about you from the start.

Was she crazy about him?

She didn't know. All those years, she'd been so focused on Javier, on getting him through adolescence safely, making sure that his future was assured. Her only thought beyond that was a vague plan to leave Cabrillo behind, to stop being the Merrill family charity case.

She smiled back, just as small, just as secret, because she just couldn't help it.

If Benedict had been anyone other than who he was— then yeah, she probably would have been crazy about him too.

Or maybe she already was.

The oven timer chimed, breaking the moment between them.

"Soup's on," Liliana yelled to the room at large.

About fifteen minutes later, they were all digging into lasagna, crusty bread, and a Caesar salad. Liliana was a great cook, which Pilar never would have guessed when she first met Liliana in high school.

Benedict was at the head of the table with Pilar at his right hand. Their knees were probably only inches apart under the table. She *could* slip her foot out of her shoe and slide it into his lap. She calculated the angles of how to do it. It would have to be her right foot, and she'd probably have to kind of cross her legs to do it—and make sure no one noticed what she was doing—but watching Benedict's efforts to keep it together while she did so would be priceless. And if she only reached his calf, he'd still jump.

She slipped her foot out of her ballet flat and—

"Did you hear that Josh is coming home soon?" Liliana asked her.

The tension at the table rose, Benedict going stiffest of all.

So much for her plan to play footsie. "I did," she said carefully, tucking her foot back into her shoe. "That's good news."

She meant it. Josh had done his time, and if he was ready to shape up, then great.

Benedict made a scornful noise. "Yeah, well, we'll see if prison actually reformed him."

Maybe yesterday's visit wasn't a smashing success. If only she'd had the chance to ask Benedict about it before this—she wasn't going to get anything meaningful out of him in front of his siblings. Not with the impenetrable-eldest-sibling role he played.

Luke set down his fork, his hands curling into fists. Uh-oh. "Maybe we should wait until he gets back before we decide to write him off?"

Whoa. She'd never seen Luke be anything but charming. He looked ready to fight.

Benedict's jaw tightened. "He's got a hell of a lot of proving to do to convince me that he's changed. Remember what he did?"

The visit *had* been bad then. And if Josh hadn't reformed, wasn't ready to be something other than a drunken waste—it wasn't a good thing he'd be getting out.

Benedict was right. Josh did have to prove himself. So why was Luke being belligerent?

"I know what he did," Luke said tightly. "And he's served his time. Maybe you should go a little easy on him instead of deciding to ride his ass from the get-go."

Her mouth dropped open. Maybe instead of lighting into Benedict, Luke could remember who the one at fault was here.

Everyone else was staring wide-eyed, limbs tense. Apparently Luke snapping at his elder brother was a surprise for everyone.

As for Benedict, his expression was coldly furious and... wounded. As if Luke had betrayed him by saying that.

Which Luke kind of had.

The silence stretched as the brothers stared each other down. Someone had to rescue the conversation here.

"How's your shoulder?" Pilar asked Penny's boyfriend. What was his name again?

"All right," he answered. He moved it in the socket. "See? Can't lift it any higher than this"—he stopped at about shoulder height—"but it's getting better. Penny helps me with my exercises."

He slid Penny a secret smile and she went pink all over. Yeah, those two were completely twitterpated.

He's been crazy about you from the start.

She slid Benedict a glance of her own. His expression had eased, wasn't so tight and angry, but now he looked resigned. And there was gratitude deep in the melancholy blue of his eyes.

He knew what she'd done, appreciated it—but seemed saddened by it.

She looked back to her plate, unable to carry the weight of his emotions and her own. The conversation went on about the boyfriend's shoulder without her as she concentrated on eating. And ignoring Benedict and how he made her feel.

Something pressed against her leg. *His leg.*

She looked up to find him smiling rather ruefully at her. He leaned close, dropped his voice—and kept his leg against hers. "I meant to ask: do you want to go for a ride after dinner?"

The sun was shining, the rain had turned everything green and bright and bursting—it sounded awesome. And finally, finally she could get him alone.

But— "I didn't bring any jeans."

Liliana, who'd been listening in, looked her up and down. "I don't think I have anything to fit you."

Nope. Liliana was tall and skinny, and Pilar... wasn't. She wasn't even going to try squeezing into Liliana's jeans. No contortion existed that would let her do that.

Benedict cleared his throat in an almost shy way. "I've, uh, got some jeans. Women's jeans," he said at her look. "They ought to fit you."

Liliana asked the question Pilar wanted to. "Why do you have women's jeans?" Only a lot louder.

Silence followed that. So much for keeping things discreet and quiet.

Benedict cleared his throat and assumed a rather impassive expression. "When I invited Pilar to dinner, I forgot to ask if she wanted to go for a ride after. And when I remembered, I decided to buy some jeans. Just in case." He made it sound reasonable, but color was creeping up his cheeks nonetheless.

It was adorable.

"I haven't ridden in years," she said, as reasonable as he. "Thank you so much for thinking of it."

She thought she heard Liliana snicker but wasn't certain.

Benedict's answering smile was all she could really take in just then. Along with the pressure of his leg, hidden from everyone except her and him.

Chapter 7

IT WAS A GOOD THING Benedict had thought to buy her some jeans, because the day was absolutely perfect for a ride. Not too hot, with a breeze blowing in from the west, the air bursting with the scent of flowers—it made Pilar happy in a deep way she hadn't been in a very long time.

Benedict was right—taking a nice long ride was a good way to clear your head.

They rode side by side on a trail that wound along the creek. The gurgle of the water joined the call of the birds in a song of spring. Neither Benedict nor Pilar said much as they rode. The silence between them must have been as comfortable for him as it was for her.

The hills were bright green, with stretches of flowers providing splashes of color in the chaparral. It looked as if an impressionist painter had taken his brush to the countryside.

They came to a stand of oaks. The ground beneath was littered with leaves and acorns, and in the middle was a flat boulder, perfect for sitting. She could imagine him and his siblings coming out here to play all the time—it was that kind of spot.

"Want to stop here for a bit?" he asked.

"Sure."

She went to sit on the rock as he tied the horses to a low-hanging branch. The sense of spring bursting out was lessened here, pushed back by the seasonless aspect of the oaks. The rock was hard and cold, sitting in the shade as it was. But when Benedict turned to her, his gaze held all the heat she would need.

He held a blanket in his hand as he stalked toward her. He snapped it out with a flick of his wrist, then crooked a finger at her. "Come here," he growled.

Oooh, caveman time. Nice.

She sauntered over, trying for slow and sassy. "Yes? Did you need something?"

He snared her about her waist and pulled her in close to him. God, but his body felt good pressed against hers.

"Aren't we supposed to be having an affair?" he asked.

"Are we?" She grinned. "Because so far you've been more talk than action."

That got him well and riled. He kissed her hard, no little peck on the corner of her mouth. And he kept on kissing her, his tongue stroking deep within her mouth even as he lowered her to the blanket. Once there, he rubbed his face into her neck, his stubble raking deliciously across her skin, making her shudder.

"You're going to leave a red mark," she protested half-heartedly.

He lifted his head, pinned her with his intent expression. "I want to. I want everyone to see."

Definitely caveman time.

An illicit thrill went through her at the thought of

wearing the mark of what they were doing, the whole town seeing it. It wasn't quiet or discreet—but she loved it.

She pulled his mouth to hers, kissing him deeply. She wanted him to mark all of her, to drive her as wild as he had in all her imaginings.

"Naked," he muttered against her mouth. "I need you naked."

Sounded good to her.

She helped him remove her shirt, boots, and jeans, managing to unbutton his shirt as she did. But when she reached for the top button of his jeans, he grabbed her wrist. Then the other. And held them over her head.

Stretched before him, completely exposed to his darkened gaze, she could only shiver as he looked her over in silence.

His free hand settled at her waist, then slid up to cup her breast. Something in his gaze opened and spilled light into the dark desire in his eyes. "I've imagined this for so long," he said huskily. "You naked, beneath me."

She tried to wriggle free of his grip, but his hand only tightened.

"Stay like that," he ordered.

She went beyond shivering at his tone—she quivered.

He released her then, secure in the knowledge that she would obey. Both of his hands went to work at her breasts. He plucked and shaped her nipples with his thumb and forefinger, then slid his hand up to take them in the webbing of his thumbs, his fingers curling into her flesh as he did. As if he couldn't bear not to have as much of her breast in his hand as he could.

And then he lowered his head and brushed his face across her breasts, dragging his stubble across the flesh, marking her there as well.

It was all delicious fire, the rub of his rough skin against her delicate parts. She groaned and tried to lift her hips, but his own kept her firmly anchored. "Please," she begged.

"Please what?" he drawled, all dark, dominant male.

She snaked a leg around his, the denim of his jeans rough against her inner thigh. She lifted her hips again, rubbing herself against his crotch, feeling her dampness spreading through the fabric.

But she kept her hands above her head, just like she'd been told.

His smile dripped with the promise of torment to come. "We'll get there." His hands slid to her belly, made an arc along the soft swell of it, traveling from hip to hip. "I love this," he said almost reverently.

Her desire dimmed. "No one likes that part of my belly."

He raised his head, did that eyebrow thing. "I didn't say I like it. I love it."

And with that she was an inferno again.

He lowered his head, rubbing his face across her belly, digging the scratchiness of his beard stubble into the softness there. He kissed and suckled at the part he said he loved, and then he sank his teeth in. Not hard enough to hurt. Just enough to say *Mine*.

She pulsed at every touch, every brush of his skin. Her clit ached. He had to touch there soon or she might die. Really, truly die. She was certain.

He set his hands at her knees and pushed, opening her to his gaze. His eyes were the dark of twilight, his mouth pursed as if seeing a treasure for the first time. He held this adoring pose for several long moments, but she didn't want to squirm or hide from it. She wanted to bask in it—so she did.

His head dipped low and she held her breath. He kissed

the inside of one thigh, then softly exhaled on the damp spot he'd left. She clenched around nothing. God, he needed to hurry. She needed his fingers in her pussy, or better yet, his cock.

He repeated the action on her other thigh and she groaned, lifting her hips greedily. He set a hand on her hipbone and pushed her back down. The pressure felt good, but not good enough.

"Patience," he rasped. "I'm gonna savor this first time. Next time we go fast. And hard."

A weird sobbing, begging noise came from her, one she'd never imagined she could make, but she was so goddamn desperate that she didn't care.

He brushed the seam of her thigh, that frontier between her leg and her sex, and every nerve ending lit up, sparks dancing under her skin. He slid both hands under her ass, cupping the globes, fingers going tight as if he couldn't believe the bounty he'd found. And then he was lifting her hips, positioning her...

Finally, he was going to put his attention where she needed it.

The first touch of his mouth was light, tentative—more of a nudge than anything else. Then a deep inhale, as if he were savoring her. His tongue traced her folds lightly, then more definitively.

She couldn't help herself; she lowered her hands to clutch at his hair, to keep him right where she needed him. As if on cue, his mouth turned hungry, devouring. His tongue flicked at her clit, his lips closing on it, and she tried to close her thighs, to hold that sensation tight. But his hands kept her wide open, made her wallow in what he was doing to her.

She scored her nails along his scalp, lifted her hips, and

he sucked harder, making fire race along her nerves. The pleasure built to a dizzying peak, stars exploding behind her eyes—and she hadn't even climaxed yet.

His fingers tightened on her thighs, his kisses becoming insistent, demanding, pushing her toward that fall that was coming. She gave in to his demands, letting the peak break over her, moaning as it rolled throughout her body, made all of her shake with it.

As she slowly sank back into reality, she was aware of him gently kissing her sex, her clit still pulsing with her release. God, but that felt good, to be lavished with caresses even after. She tugged at his hair, bringing his mouth to hers, tasting herself on his tongue. His erection rubbed insistently between them, reminding her that it was his turn now.

She pushed him back onto his knees, peering up at him from under her lashes as she unzipped his fly. His breathing went all shuddery as she rubbed him through his boxers, intending to torment him as much as he had her.

She freed his cock once his breathing was ragged enough to please her. Thick and long, it really was a magnificent work of art. Almost as magnificent as the man it was attached to. She brushed her cheek along it, savoring the silken feel of it, the scent of his arousal rising from the curls surrounding it.

A bead appeared at the tip and she used her thumb to rub it around, gripping the length of him tightly, her fingers just barely meeting.

Enough teasing. This was torment for her too.

She took the length of him as deeply as she could within her mouth, too hungry for the taste of him, the fullness of him, to do it slowly. He groaned, his hips jerking slightly, and she sensed his hand hovering at her head.

She pulled back. "You can hold my head."

He sank his hands into her hair, pulling tight and angling her head. "Even like this?"

It felt wickedly good. She liked his caveman side. "Yes," she breathed.

"Tell me if it hurts."

"I won't break."

"No, but if I hurt you, I might."

She had no time to process how that made her feel because his cock was nudging at her lips, and as soon as she let him, he was plunging deeply, his hand in her hair holding her steady. His other hand drifted along her cheeks and jaw, gently caressing her, and the contrast between that and the rough grip on her hair, his fierce thrusts into her mouth, made her desire rise all over again, her thighs going slippery with it.

Suddenly he released her, pulling his cock free. He pulled her up to her knees, staring intently at her.

"What's wrong?" she asked, her heart going a mile a minute. He certainly seemed to be enjoying it if his growly groans were anything to go by. Not to mention the wild movement of his hips.

"I don't want to come in your mouth," he said low and rough. "I want to come inside you."

Yes. They should totally do that. She leaned back, pulled him down on her. "There are condoms in my jeans. I learned my lesson the last time."

He laughed, then shook his head. "I wanted my first time with you to be in a bed."

Now she had to laugh. Poor Benedict and his need to romance her. "You can fuck me in a bed later."

His eyes darkened.

"But if you don't fuck me right now"—she reached

between them and squeezed his erection, making him groan —"I'm going to be really pissed."

He didn't need any more convincing. He went for the condoms, rolled one on, and settled himself between her thighs. His jeans were rough against her skin, his cock smooth and hard as it nudged against her pussy.

He took his time sinking into her. The expression on his face... it almost hurt to look at him. Instead, she concentrated on the sensation of him filling her, her legs tightening about him, their hips coming to rest against each other. His breath, hot in her ear, the drag of her nipples against the fabric of his shirt. All the physical things between them— and not the emotions written on his face.

But then he began to move, and as she met him, she couldn't look away. She was caught in his gaze, in the open adoration there.

He looked as if he'd been granted his heart's desire. She certainly couldn't look away as Benedict turned that expression on her.

That expression—more than the slick glide of their flesh together, more than the way his pelvis rubbed just right against her clit—sent her sliding to yet another orgasm, all of her clenching around him as he tossed her over the edge.

He followed right behind, his cock pulsing as he came hard within her, just like he'd wanted to.

They crumpled into each other, both of them breathing heavily. She savored his weight, ran a hand through his damp hair, licked at the salty sweat on his neck. She slowly noticed he was... not exactly trembling. More like a little earthquake was going off beneath his skin.

She felt the exact same way.

"I wish I could ask you to stay," he said into her hair.

She stiffened.

"I won't though," he went on. "I just want to enjoy the time I have left with you."

Benedict suffers in silence. He wouldn't ask her to stay, which was probably for the best. Because in this moment, she'd seriously consider saying yes.

His little gestures toward her—dealing with the tires, ordering her lunch, taking her to church, fixing her sink—they didn't feel like charity right now. They felt like love.

In her heart of hearts, she wanted that love. And that scared her because she could lose herself in loving Benedict.

He rolled off her, tucking her along his side. "Are you cold?"

"Nope. You make a good blanket." She ran her hand along his chest. "Are you ready to talk about your visit with Josh?"

He went rigid, then sighed. "Josh looked harder, leaner than I expected. Prison's whittled him down."

"Mmm." She tangled her fingers in his chest hair and waited for him to go on.

"I asked him what he was going to do when he got out. Turns out that Liliana's already told him he can work in the stockyard, without asking me."

"He'll need a job."

"He'd better not fuck it up. He's had all the chances he's going to get from me."

A chill moved across her skin. He was right to not trust Josh, not until he'd proven himself, but he spoke so coldly about it. "Do you ever regret what you said to him? Before he went to prison?"

"No." Flat. Stark. "The alternative would have been to sit back and watch him go to hell."

"Some might say he ended up there anyway." She couldn't quite say why she was trying to defend Josh, even as weakly as she was, but she wanted Benedict to give just slightly on this. To drop the hard-ass routine—if only for a moment.

His hand stroked her hair, his expression tight as he pondered that. "I think about it a lot," he said finally, "what I could have done differently, what might have saved him. And I never come up with a good answer. After this last stunt—that girl with him in the car? She barely survived. I decided I was done trying to catch him. Let him fall and see if that teaches him better. And if not, then nothing will."

She pondered that. "I don't think I'm ready to stop trying to catch Javier."

"You'll have to one day."

"He'll be on his own two feet then. And he won't be in danger of falling."

Benedict could tell her to let Javier go to hell on his own —and he might have slightly selfish reasons for it—but Javier wasn't Josh. Her brother just needed the right kind of push to fall into the life she wanted for him. And she was going to keep pushing until she found it.

But they had been talking of Benedict's brother. "Was Josh at least happy to see you?"

He snorted. "No. He went on about making amends for what he'd done, which sounded good at first..."

"But?"

"But then he said he had to go find Leonora, to make amends to her."

Leonora Harper: the girlfriend Josh had almost killed.

"Does she want to see him?"

"I don't know," Benedict admitted. "I told Josh if she doesn't want to talk to him then she shouldn't have to. He can't force an apology on her." A deep exhale. "Josh said I could never understand since I've never apologized for a goddamn thing in my life."

She pressed a kiss to his throat, at the base of it, where it met his chest. His pulse fluttered under her lips.

He laughed without humor. "The rest of the visit went about the same."

"What did your dad and Liliana say?"

"Liliana didn't say anything. Just looked kind of shocked. Maybe a little disapproving, I don't know. But Dad…" His fingers twisted in her hair but didn't hurt her. His voice went low. "Dad said that while I might be handling the company well, I didn't know how to handle Josh."

How that must have hurt him. She could hear the pain now in the fractures in his tone. She pressed a kiss to his chest this time, right above his heart.

"He's right," Benedict admitted. "I don't know how to handle Josh."

That fell like a weight upon them. Perhaps he'd never be able to help Josh. Perhaps she'd never get through to Javier. Perhaps the two of them were doomed to watch their younger brothers slide into self-destruction.

She couldn't think of anything that would ease the pain for either of them, so she kept silent.

He released his grip on her hair, pressed his lips there instead. "Before you," he said, "I wouldn't have had anyone to talk this over with."

Something tore within her. God, he didn't have to ask her to stay—not when he confessed things like that. She'd stay just to save him from his self-imposed loneliness.

And what of her plans for herself?

For all that Benedict was lonely, he'd chosen this. Chosen to be the strong, silent type, managing everything around him.

She hadn't chosen to raise Javier. She was doing her best —which wasn't great—but she still wanted something for herself.

Did that make her selfish?

"Am I wrong to want to leave?"

His breath arrested in that beautiful chest.

God, he *did* think her selfish. He'd never do such a thing. He'd hang on till the bitter end, no matter how Javier pushed him away.

"No," he said finally.

The relief that moved through her was crushing. It was terrible to be so dependent on his good opinion. But she was now. Had always been.

He lifted himself over her, and the blue of his eyes was the blue of the sea where it met the horizon. Far and melancholy. "I want you to be happy," he said. "And if leaving makes you happy, you should do it."

But what if it would make me happier to stay?

She didn't ask, because she didn't know. And it would be cruel to nurture his hopes like that.

He's crazy about you.

She had no idea what was right or what she wanted in the future. All she knew was that she wanted to hold him close now.

So she did, pressing her face into the comforting darkness of his chest and simply breathing him in.

The future could wait.

Chapter 8

"YOU LIVE IN THE POOL HOUSE?"

Pilar hadn't meant it to come out like that, but Benedict only smiled and squeezed her hand. Which he'd been holding since they'd left the barn, tiptoeing past the main house as they made their way toward his place. She'd never have guessed that he was afraid of his younger siblings, but the roundabout path he'd taken—very much out of sight of the big house—proved that he was. Or at least that he was afraid of meeting them after sexing up Pilar outdoors.

"I like that it's smaller," he said. "Gives me more privacy."

"Yeah, I can imagine that having Liliana and Luke around puts a cramp in your style," she said, nudging him playfully.

"I've never brought a woman here."

She gave him the side eye.

"I'm not a monk," he protested. "I'd rather go to her place. And then I can leave whenever I want."

A bitter taste flooded her mouth. Jealousy? That was silly since he'd just said he never brought women here. And she wasn't a nun herself. She'd had to be discreet so that Javier wouldn't notice, but discreet didn't mean celibate.

"Don't worry," she said with fake lightness, "I won't overstay my welcome. I'll just change and get out of your hair."

Before she could even blink, he'd spun her around and was kissing her fiercely. "The hell you will," he growled against her mouth.

Okay, maybe her jealousy was uncalled for.

"But I need a shower," she said, slow and seductive.

He gave her a wicked smile. "I've got a shower here. You can even use mine."

She batted her lashes at him. "Oh, the guest bathroom is fine. Does the pool house have a guest bathroom?"

"It does." He nipped at her earlobe, sending shivers through her. "But mine is nicer."

"Show me."

Once she was in his house, she could see all the things that were missing from his austere office. Family portraits, plants, books everywhere. Even some books in Spanish, which surprised her more than it should have. Everything was still organized within an inch of its life—but this was his life. Right here in front of her.

He stood by the front door, watching her warily as she took it all in. "It's uh..." He rubbed the back of his neck.

He hadn't been kidding about not bringing women back here.

"Generally in situations like this you say, 'I'm sorry it's such a mess.'" She did another survey of the room. "But that won't work here."

Finally he came close to her. "No. How about 'Come see my bathroom.'"

"That'll work."

She discovered that *nice* didn't even begin to cover his

bathroom. There must have been acres of white marble in this bathroom, with a huge shower that had at least five showerheads, all placed at various points along the wall. This shower was the very definition of decadence.

And the tub! "Are there jets?" she asked incredulously. A person could comfortably swim laps in there.

All this was just in the pool house. She couldn't even imagine what the bathrooms in the main house looked like.

She turned her wide-eyed gaze on him. "This is amazing."

He burst out laughing. "Don't think it came this way. I had the bathroom remodeled when I moved in. I'm a sucker for a nice bathroom."

She winked at him. "So am I. And you never answered me: are those jets?"

"Yep. Want to try it?"

Of course she did. But...

She bit her lip, crossed her arms over her chest. If she did this, she knew where it would end: with both of them falling hard. Her most of all.

She only had to say no and he'd back away. She could leave in three months, heart intact. Or at least mostly intact.

But God, she wanted to sleep with him. Not just fuck him—sleep with him. Wanted to bury her nose into the crook of his neck, smell the sun-warmed skin, curve close to him under the silk sheets of his too-large bed all night long.

"Yes," she said finally. "I do."

Everything became weighted then. His movements as he started the water, her gaze as she followed him. His hands as he lifted them to the hem of her shirt and pulled it from her. His breath as he stared at her exposed torso.

"Pilar." He made music of her name, of the rolling

consonants and stretched vowels. No one else had ever done that.

"I'm here."

He pulled her into his body and kissed her like he was starving, even as his hand worked at the fastening of her bra.

When he was done, she crossed her arms over her chest. Not out of any shyness, but because it seemed right to prolong the revelation of herself, although he'd seen it all before.

But it still seemed new.

He flicked open the button of her jeans, crouched to pull them from her legs. She stepped out, but he stayed where he was, staring up at her, her arms still crossed. Covered by her limbs and a scrap of fabric, yet completely exposed.

His thumbs hooked into the waistband of her panties, dragging them to the floor. Her hands fell away from her chest—and she was completely uncovered.

He straightened, and she caught a glimpse of them in the mirror. Him, completely covered, and her, hidden by him, a pale thigh, a bare arm peeping from behind him.

He caught her by the hand, pulled her toward the tub. She felt like Venus as she stepped in, limbs sliding beneath the water to become blurred and perfect.

He knelt beside the tub, switched on the jets. The water churned. She couldn't help herself—she ducked beneath the surface, the jets gently pummeling her, turning every-thing around her to bubbles.

She came up with a laugh, blinking water out of her eyes and spluttering with pure happiness.

If she had a tub like this, she'd soak in it every day. And twice on Sundays. It was heat and pressure and silken, perfumed luxury... all she needed was a glass of wine and a good book.

Oh, and a big strappy cowboy naked and wet in here with her.

She looked him up and down; he was still entirely too clothed. "Aren't you getting in?"

"I thought you'd never ask," he said dryly.

She flicked water at him. "Of course you were invited."

He shucked his clothes and slid in behind her, his thighs hard under hers, his chest solid against her back, and his erection pressing into her ass. His arms slid around her belly, his mouth nuzzling into the skin of her neck.

She felt sexy, wanted, and cherished. She could really get used to this. Even more frightening, she *wanted* to get used to this.

He pulled a washcloth from the stack of towels next to the tub. It was as fluffy as a chenille throw, not ratty and too-much laundered like her washcloths. He swirled it in the tub, the water dancing languorously with his motions, then he soaped it and set it to her shoulders. Down her arm, slow as sin, carefully attending to each finger when he reached her hand. Then back again to her shoulders, across to her other arm to give it the same treatment. Up again, where he hovered at the junction of her neck and shoulder.

Decision time. He could go down her back, stroking the washcloth to just above her ass, then up again.

Or his hand could slide forward to scrub her breasts.

Either way was fine, and she was sure he was going to lavish every inch of her with attention, so she really had no preference—

He nudged her forward. Her back then. She wasn't disappointed. Only frustrated.

"We want to make certain all of you is squeaky clean," he rumbled into her ear.

He was tormenting her on purpose. Once she got him into that bed, she'd return the favor.

He rubbed slow circles on her back, then the washcloth slipped around her waist to travel up her belly. He slid it between her breasts, lifting one with his free hand.

He found her nipple, the washcloth ignored as he kneaded and teased until she was panting, her hips lifting, twisting, with her wishing his hips were there to anchor hers.

"Slow, baby, slow," he said. "I want to savor this."

Torment her was more like it.

He released her breasts, tapped her leg. She lifted it out of the water, and he swiped from her thighs all the way to her toes. His arms were so long he hardly even had to strain. He could enclose her entirely in his body like this, every inch of her protected by him.

He did the other leg, then paused.

"Haven't you forgotten a spot?" she reminded him.

"Have I?" He found the line of tendon running from her shoulder to her neck and took it in his teeth, just hard enough to make all of her clench. "Whoops."

His hand without the washcloth slipped between her legs. It trailed along her inner thigh and stopped right before he reached her pussy lips.

"Here?" he asked. "Did I forget to wash here?"

She shook her head. "Higher."

His fingers moved not even an eighth of an inch. "Here?"

She lifted her hips, forcing his fingers where she wanted them. "There."

He released a deep breath. He traced her folds, learning them as carefully as he'd learned the rest of her.

His thumb found her clit and pressed, sensation bursting from that spot to bathe all of her in pleasure. He slid one thick finger inside her, then another—stretched her deliciously, all the while circling her clit. She pulsed with his every touch, every bit of her straining toward her climax. He pulled his fingers into a come-hither motion, hitting a spot deep within—and she came in a great guttering rush, a knot tightening then coming completely untied with her release.

Different than the releases he'd given her earlier with his mouth and his cock. But just as good.

Oh yes, she could definitely get used to this.

"Your turn," she told him and wriggled about so that she was astride him. His erection nudged insistently at her sex, as eager as she was to get on with the next bit.

But the man himself held back. "Let's move to the bed," he suggested. "I kind of... I've imagined you in that bed. A lot."

He bit his lower lip, looking so damn adorable her heart might crack right in two. She couldn't say no to that face.

"Let's go to the bed then."

He rose, water sluicing from his length, tucked his arms behind her back and knees and straight up just lifted her.

"Whoa!" She set a hand to his shoulder. "I'm too—"

He stopped her with a kiss. "Don't you dare say too heavy."

She supposed she wasn't—not for him at least. "Okay."

He set her down long enough to pull a robe around himself and wrap a towel around her, then he was lifting her again and heading for the bedroom.

He tossed her onto the bed, and she bounced as she hit, the first time she'd bounced on a bed since she was a kid. She couldn't help but giggle.

The bed was soft as a cloud, the duvet silky—decadence. Pure decadence.

She had only a moment to appreciate it before he was over her, kissing her so deeply, so hungrily. He shrugged out of his robe as she wriggled out of the towel, the two of them trying never to break their kiss.

They mostly succeeded.

He braced himself above her, his shoulders broad, the tension in the muscles of his arms delightful to see. He'd lifted her as if she weighed nothing with those arms. She ran her hands over them—so taut, the muscles bulging.

"Impressed?" he rumbled.

"Did you do all those biceps curls just for me?"

He laughed, then gave her a swift kiss on the corner of her mouth. "Yep. Thought of you through every rep." His expression went serious. "Thought of you a lot." He reached between them, finding her clit again. "Thought of you like this, naked on my bed, me rubbing you just like this."

She panted as the pleasure built, quicker than ever before. The man was frighteningly good at giving her orgasms. "You have a very good imagination," she got out.

"This is better than imaginings."

She caught at his hand. "No. I want you inside me. Now."

She wanted him with her in this, not on the outside, looking at her worshipfully.

He stared at her for a moment, the weight of it almost too much to bear. Then he was reaching for a condom, sliding it on—and he was with her. Fully. Completely.

"God, you're big," she moaned. Of course she knew that —he'd been inside her not more than an hour ago—but somehow she had to tell him that.

He halted, those impressive arms holding him over her. "Am I hurting you?"

So caring, so conscientious it almost made her ache. "No, it's great," she assured him. "It's awesome."

It would be even better when he started moving.

He withdrew, then thrust forward, grinding her against his pubic bone as he did.

"Jesus," she hissed.

He did it again and again, his face a study in determined concentration, his every thrust a buzzer shock to her clit. Her toes curled, all of her tensing under the onslaught. She could not possibly be coming again, but she was, pleasure shuddering through her in great, shaking waves.

When she could finally think again—could see again—he was paused above her, watching her.

And still hard as a rock, nestled tightly within her.

"Aren't you... aren't you finished?" she asked. Did he do that tantric yoga? How could he not have climaxed with her?

"No," he gritted, the lines of his neck taut and stark. Without warning, he withdrew and flipped her to her stomach, raising her hips into the air and exposing her sex to him.

"Grab the headboard," he ordered.

Her fingers curled around the slats, obeying him before her mind had even begun to consider it. She pressed her cheek against the pillow, rubbed her breasts against the sheets, and raised her ass high, sensing that he wanted her just like this.

He ran a hand along her back, a connoisseur appreciating a particularly lovely bit of sculpture. His fingers slid across the globes of her ass, sinking into the flesh there for one delicious moment. Then his knees were between hers, nudging her thighs apart. Opening her for him.

His cock teased at her pussy, his hair-roughened thighs

brushing against hers. Her hands tightened on the headboard.

"So beautiful," he whispered. "I've wanted to fuck you over my desk for... for forever."

All of her pulsed, and she rubbed her nipples against the sheets, needing that friction.

"It's all I've thought about for years," he continued. "You in those sexy, teasing clothes of yours. Your pouty lips. I'd shove your skirt up to your waist, tear off your panties, and fuck you until you screamed."

She felt close to screaming just from his description. His fingers dug into her hips, and he thrust forward, his cock stretching her until almost the breaking point. It was so carnal she had to moan.

"Do you feel this?" he demanded as he thrust again. "It's all for you." He fisted his hand in her hair, like before, but without hurting. Just holding her oh so tightly.

She was in the most submissive position she could imagine, but she felt only worshipped. Adored.

"This cock"—another hard thrust, one she had to push back against lest she slam into the headboard—"this"—his hand left her hair, pinched her nipple, all of her clenching at the pressure—"it's all for you."

He leaned into her ear, his thrusts growing faster, wilder, even as his hand slid down her belly. "I can give you more," he promised darkly. His fingers slid through her curls and found her clit, pleasure sparking through her brain. "I can give you everything."

They came together then, her clenching around him as his cock jerked within her, both of them shaking with their release, the bone-melting satisfaction of it.

They slumped together onto the bed, his weight heavy and reassuring. And right. He breathed harshly into her ear, and she savored the sensation, his weight and breath and skin surrounding her on one side while the silken softness of his bed supported her on the other.

She wanted to do this again. Wanted to do it every night and every morning.

Sadness curled within her, as light as a thread of smoke and just as acrid.

She could. She could turn to him and tell him what was in her heart. If he felt the same—and she suspected he did —he'd do the romantic thing.

He'd ask her to marry him.

She could go from being his housekeeper's daughter to recipient of his family's scholarship and his charity secretary, all the way on up to being his wife.

Would it be so bad, standing by this man's side for a lifetime?

"What are you thinking about?" he murmured into her ear.

No, it would be no hardship to stay with a man who treated her as he did. Who read her as well as he did.

"Nothing," she said. "You finally wore me out."

Humor was always her shield against him, but this wasn't the time to ponder all of her feelings for him and her desires for her future. Nothing needed to be decided at this moment.

He took care of the condom, then came back to tuck her against him, pulling the sheet over the both of them.

"Wait," she said. There was one last thing she wanted to do. "Roll onto your back."

He did as she asked, watching her intently. She laid her hand over his eyes. She couldn't do this if he were staring at her like that. "Eyes closed, please," she asked primly, feeling his lashes flutter against her palm.

When she lifted her hand, his eyes stayed shut, although a smile teased at the corner of his mouth. She pulled the sheet completely free of his body, now laid out for her, just as she'd wanted.

She started at his feet, long boned with high arches. Sturdy feet to carry a man through all his days without faltering. His toes ever so subtly curled and uncurled, as if squirming under her scrutiny.

She ran her hands along his calves heavy with muscle and found the bare patches where his boots rubbed. A tiny thing, but hers now, since she'd found them and claimed them, just as he'd claimed that corner of her mouth as his.

Up now to his knees, knobby and not particularly attractive. But they were part of him, which made them dear to her. And on to the thick muscles girding his thighs, the kind that left deep dents along the side of his legs as he flexed. A lovely divot there for her to run her fingers over.

And then the center of him, his cock lying quiet and soft, his sac heavy, nestled in the hair that was perfumed with their lovemaking.

Her fingers went *tip tip tip* along the ridges of his abdomen, which she suspected he was flexing for her. She ran her fingertips up and down, appreciating the show.

He let out a small laugh when she hit a sensitive spot.

Ticklish, hmm? She'd have to test that again later.

She slid both hands up his chest, her fingers catching in the hair there. Then along his shoulders, so broad, so strong, and down his arms. Until she found his fingers and linked her own with them tightly.

"You can open your eyes," she whispered.

When he did, they were the blue of dawn, lit with promise. He squeezed her hands, still joined with his. "Stay with me tonight."

As if she could do anything but. She'd meant to take out these feelings for him later, to come to a decision slowly, rationally.

But then she'd run her hands over every inch of him and found herself already decided.

"Of course I will."

He pulled her down to him, tucking her alongside him before drawing the sheet up. "Good," he said. "I want to wake next to you."

She wanted nothing more than that herself. Although it was still light out, she found herself suddenly exhausted.

She yawned widely as his arm tightened around her. Her eyes wouldn't stay open another moment, not if her life depended on it.

And with his arm around her, the both of them limp and satisfied, she fell asleep.

Chapter 9

SOMETHING SMELLED WONDERFUL.

Pilar breathed deeply, still three-quarters asleep. But that scent—warm and sleepy and male—it compelled her to wake. It curled in her nose, tugged her toward awareness. She snuggled closer, her nose and lips meeting hot skin. She pushed the tip of tongue past her lips, stealing a taste of that skin. Salt and musk. Yum.

She shifted. Or tried to. She was pinned between his heavy thighs, his arm anchoring her waist. That was almost as nice as his scent surrounding her. She could get used to waking up with him as a blanket.

She opened one eye. It was dark out, not even a hint of morning light. She had a few more hours with him then, before she'd have to head home to shower and dress and appear to be nothing more than his secretary.

And after five p.m. what would happen?

Things had shifted between them today. Or yesterday. Whenever it was. He might claim that everything would be as before at work, but there would be at least a frisson between them, a new awareness of the other.

Leaving was infinitely more complicated, especially since she wasn't entirely sure she wanted to.

Briiiing.

The ring of her phone had her coming completely awake, shoving aside her introspective mood. No one called at this hour for anything good.

She pushed Benedict's arm away, wriggled out from beneath his leg. He made a noise of protest, but she ignored it.

Her phone. Where was her phone?

Briiing.

She searched the floor beside her, watching intently for the glow of the screen.

If it was in her purse... She went to turn to find it, to search there—no, there the phone was. Just under her shirt.

She scrabbled for it, praying she wasn't too late, that she could answer in time.

Eleven thirty-two, the display read.

Definitely bad news.

She hit Answer and brought the phone to her ear. "Hello?"

There was silence on the other end. Probably only half a second's worth, but just long enough for her to be aware of Benedict sitting up behind her. Of him coming close to her.

Long enough for her to get really, really worried at what she was about to hear.

"Hello. Is this Pilar Lopez?"

Shit. The woman sounded very official.

Don't be the hospital. Or the coroner.

Speak. She had to speak. "Yes, that's me." Amazing, how steady her voice sounded.

"Are you Javier Lopez's sister?"

Fuck. That was the last thing she wanted to hear.

She dropped her face into her free hand. Benedict clasped her shoulder, kneading gently.

"Yes. I am." The steadiness was leaking out of her voice.

"I'm Officer Tait from the sheriff's office."

Pilar's heart felt as if it were sloshing about in her chest. *Don't let it be that bad, don't let it be that bad—*

"I'm calling because your brother was arrested for shoplifting."

HAVING Benedict take her to the station was maybe a bad idea. But he'd insisted and she'd been grateful for it. At first.

As they neared the station, his calm support had hardened into something brittle. He was tense, stiff, the lines of his expression set into something vaguely frightening. As if he was furious and trying to hold it in.

But Benedict drove as calmly, as capably as ever. Thank God.

The night seemed too dark with no moon, no streetlights, and only the headlights of the truck to mark their way. And Benedict, so silent beside her, his tension a physical thing filling the cab of the truck, combining with her own anxiety to make the atmosphere thick, toxic.

When they'd pulled into the station and the truck was parked and off, she turned to him. "You can stay here."

What she meant was he *should* stay there. She couldn't carry his tension and her own. He meant well of course, but she could handle this by herself. After all, she'd been solely responsible for Javier for five years now.

"I can't let you go alone," he said, his words heavier than they should have been.

She wondered why she'd even tried. Of course he would come.

"Okay." She grabbed for the door handle.

"Wait. I'll open it."

The time it took him to come around to her door was interminable. She had nothing to do but wait and think on Javier's situation. And worry—which she'd already been doing on the drive over. She wanted to act, to grab the door, to march into the station and figure out what was wrong.

She waited for Benedict instead.

They walked to the door in silence, the air cold with spring chill, and as he opened it for her, the awful realization hit her.

Benedict Merrill was escorting her to the sheriff's office in the dead of night so she could bail out her brother.

The gossip was going to be worse than she'd ever endured. Maybe even worse than he'd ever endured. There was no *quiet* or *discreet* after this. Not that there might have been after their time together today—but there was really no going back after this.

She snuck a glance up at him as he held open the door, his arm as hard as an iron bar. But he wouldn't look at her. His face was tight, his expression closed.

If he was regretting coming with her—regretting starting an affair with her—it was too late now.

She walked through the door, going for the front desk where a middle-aged man in uniform sat.

"I'm here to..."

She faltered, the right word not coming to her lips. *See my brother? Bail out my brother? Rescue my brother?*

"I was told my brother is here," she finished. "Javier Lopez."

The officer typed something into the computer, his

movements easy. No doubt this was just another Sunday night on duty for him.

Shame swamped her that she should be standing here, waiting for this man to take her to her brother and that he should be bored by it all.

"Yep, there he is," the officer said, never looking up from the computer. "Shoplifting."

How petty and stupid it sounded. What a dumb thing to do.

She was going to kill Javier when he came out.

The officer kept tapping at the computer. "The store is still deciding whether or not to press charges."

"He hasn't been charged?" There was a little bit of hope. *Please let the store drop this.*

"Not yet," the officer confirmed. Rawlings, his nametag read. "I'll take you to him." As he rose, he caught sight of Benedict and stilled.

Did he recognize Benedict? Or was he simply going to forbid Benedict from coming along?

Officer Rawlings's gaze stayed on Benedict for just a beat too long and then slid away, his face tightening with embarrassment.

He did recognize Benedict. And Rawlings was embarrassed for him.

Perfect. That extra dollop of disdain was just perfect. And that would be the start of the gossip.

"Follow me," the officer ordered.

Javier sat in a holding cell by himself, shoulders slumped almost to the floor. It was all wrong to see him behind bars in that dingy, industrial-green box. A surge of pity and protectiveness rose within her. She should have stopped this somehow.

Now she had to make it right.

Javier raised his head as they approached, his eyes red, but dry. Poor kid.

He said nothing as they approached, only watched warily. And she might have imagined it, but did his eyes harden when he saw Benedict?

Javier wouldn't dare pick a fight. Not in this situation. Please God.

"What happened?" she asked. Neutral. Calm. She would get them through this.

Javier chewed on his lip for a moment, then shrugged, trying for bravado. "They think I stole some stuff, but I didn't, there was nothing on me—"

"Hang on." She held up a hand. "Start from the beginning."

He blinked and his lip trembled a hair.

"Take a breath," she said, heartened by this show of emotion from him. He was no criminal. There must have been some kind of mistake. "Take your time. We're not in a rush."

Benedict might have flinched beside her, but she couldn't be certain. Besides, Javier needed her attention, not him.

"Eduardo and I were in the store, looking at some work boots." Javier's voice held a hint of the little boy he'd once been, tugging at her heart.

And yet...

"Work boots?" she asked. "You don't work."

But those pants in his room, the ones that he shouldn't have been able to afford—those were work pants. A terrible suspicion began to form in her mind. One she didn't want to allow purchase.

She wrapped her arms around herself, wishing she'd

thought to bring a jacket. It was so cold in here. And stuffy. It stank of grease and sweat and fear. She wriggled her nose to try to clear out that smell.

Javier didn't answer her question. "We didn't buy anything," he said, "but as we were leaving, the security guard stopped us, asked if he could check our pockets. We said no, there wasn't anything in them. Then he said that there had been a lot of thefts lately and that the suspects fit our description."

She knew where this was going. A teenager who looked like Javier, with his sullen attitude—boys like him were often the first suspects.

And yet—there had been those expensive pants in his room. How had he paid for those? He said they'd been looking at work boots...

She didn't want the accusations to be true. But wanting wouldn't make them false if he'd done it.

"Did the police search you when they came?" she asked.

"Yeah." He almost rolled his eyes. Well, at least his attitude was intact.

"Did they find anything?"

"No! I just said I didn't take anything."

Benedict crossed his arms, and she could no longer ignore the disbelief in his stance. But she would have to deal with that later, once she got Javier out of this cell.

"Okay," she said slowly, "the police didn't find anything, but they still arrested you—"

"You don't believe me," Javier burst out. "You never believe me."

They could not have this fight here. Not in the middle of the sheriff's office with bars between them. And not with Benedict and Officer Rawlings watching.

Time to take Javier home. She could figure things out better there.

She turned to the officer. "Is he free to go?"

"Yep." The man unlocked the cell as uncaringly as he'd done everything else. No doubt he'd seen worse family arguments here.

She just wished it hadn't been *her* family argument.

"Let's get out of here," Benedict said under his breath. His first words since they'd walked in.

She sighed. "Come on, Javier."

He didn't need to be told twice. He was out of the cell and going for the front entrance before she'd finished. But no matter how fast he ran, they'd have to come back since the legal issues were far from resolved. For now though, she only had to get her brother home.

The night was colder than she remembered, instantly raising goose bumps on her arms. She rubbed at them, but the cold seeped through anyway.

Javier was waiting under the harsh spotlight by the front door, his head down and his lip curled. He was trying for tough, but he just looked young. Still so young.

And so stupid.

"How could you get arrested?" she snapped.

He went even sulkier, all of him closing off. "You heard the cops. I didn't have anything on me."

Benedict came to stand near them, just outside the reach of the light, making it impossible for her to see his expression.

She turned her focus back on Javier, the only one who mattered in all this. "And those work pants in your room? Oh yes," she said at his look of shock, "I found those. How did you afford them?"

"You think I stole those?"

"What else am I supposed to think? You don't have a job."

He dropped his head and muttered something to the sidewalk.

"What?" she asked.

"I got a job," he practically shouted this time.

"What? Where? How did you do that?"

A job? How could he have gotten a job? He was supposed to be in school.

"I'm eighteen," her brother grumbled. "I don't need your permission."

"Watch it," Benedict growled, shifting menacingly in the shadows.

She held up a hand to him. This was between her and Javier.

"Where is this job?" If it was anything illegal...

"It's at Ángel's shop," Javier admitted.

"A car shop." All that work to save, to get him an education, to clear his path to college... "You want to work on cars?"

Wow, that was shrill. But she was so pissed she was literally shaking, the cold banished by the anger rising in her.

"I'm not actually working on the cars, just cleaning up, fetching parts. But I'm learning so much just watching him." And for the first time since she could remember, Javier looked happy. Interested in something.

Still. "You want to work on cars?" she repeated.

This wasn't the way it was supposed to be. Damn it, he couldn't do this.

"No, it's building cars!" he protested. "It's an art."

"It's not a career."

"You went to college! Where's your career?" Javier

gestured at Benedict, his mouth twisting into a sneer. "You just take his notes and fetch him coffee."

She took a sharp breath, the cold rushing back in to coat her skin.

He was right. All those years of school, of working toward what she'd wanted—and she was only Benedict's secretary.

She had the sudden sense of something large crumbling about her, suffocating her with the dust from the rubble.

Javier wasn't going to college—and she had been *this* close to taking back her resignation. *This* close to spending her entire life under Benedict Merrill's shadow.

Everything was turning out exactly how she didn't want it to.

"That's enough," Benedict snapped at her brother. He stepped into the light and stabbed a finger toward his truck. "Get your ass in there and work on your apology to your sister."

She didn't even try to stop Benedict. How could she, when she felt numb all over? She rubbed at her arms again, dimly noting the prickles of her goose bumps, the quivering of her limbs.

Why hadn't she brought a jacket again?

And how was she going to fix this? Oh God, how could she ever fix any of this? She rubbed harder, barely feeling her own skin beneath her palms.

"Pilar."

Benedict was calling her, but it wasn't gentle. It was harsh and almost *mean*.

"What?" Amazing that her mouth still worked. She could hardly feel her lips.

"You need to let him fall."

That snapped her right out of it.

"Let him fall?" She narrowed her eyes at him, anger bubbling through her veins. Which was certainly better than the numbness.

No, Javier wasn't falling on this one—not when the cops hadn't even found anything on him.

"Yes," Benedict said. "It's the only way he'll learn."

"Learn what? That he can be punished for shoplifting when he didn't have any stolen stuff?" Of course Benedict couldn't see how unfair that was. He'd never even set a toe wrong.

He turned his head, the light only illuminating half his face. But that half could have been carved from stone. "The punishment won't be so bad. And it'll get his head right. Isn't that what you want?"

She did, but not like this. "And if he didn't do it?" she countered. "He's an adult. This will go on his record."

"He needs it." Firm. Final. A judge pronouncing a sentence. "You heard how he spoke to you."

"He's mad, and he's a teenager," she said, exasperated. "He's not Josh."

That... that might have been a blow too far. His face went ghastly in the harsh light, his expression sagging.

But she was *right*: Javier wasn't Josh. He hadn't done anything near as bad.

"I never said he was," Benedict ground out.

"But you want me to punish him as if he were."

He didn't deny it. He just stood there, trapped in the beam of the spotlight, jaw clenching.

"How many cars did Josh smash up before that final crash?" She pressed on. "How many DUIs, bar fights, did you guys cover up for him?" She didn't need him to answer that. She already knew—a lot. And he knew that she knew.

"And you want me to come down hard on Javier this first time? For shoplifting?"

She didn't add the bit about Javier not having any stolen items. She didn't need to. Benedict's silence—still, all encompassing—told her she'd more than hit her mark. That there was no farther to dig.

She'd cut as deeply as she could.

He stared off at nothing, his expression stark, his breathing harsh. And never saying anything.

Finally, she shook her head. "You don't get a do-over with my brother."

That broke the spell holding him. He blinked as if clearing away a fog, and his face twisted into something perilously close to hatred.

It made her blood turn to ice, that expression she'd never seen before on him.

"You're right." That wasn't Benedict's voice, not that cold, harsh thing. How could it be coming from his throat? "I'm sorry. I won't interfere again."

There was something terribly final to the words, as if he were really saying *I won't bother to care again.*

Now that she knew how much she craved his care —*loved* his care—it hurt. More than hurt. It *ached.*

Her knees wobbled, shuddered with the shivers wracking her, but she couldn't collapse here in front of the sheriff's office. She had to get Javier home and then figure a way out of this mess for him.

And then... and then Javier would graduate, just as she'd planned, and she'd leave. Just as she'd planned.

She could fix all of this. There was still a chance.

She climbed into the truck with shaky legs, thankful that Benedict didn't try to help her in. He said he wouldn't interfere any longer, and he'd hold to it.

Javier was silent and small in the back seat. No mention was made of the apology Benedict thought he owed her.

Benedict said nothing at all. He drove them home in silence, dropped them off in silence.

She wondered if he might never speak to her again.

Chapter 10

PILAR WAS ALL COLD EFFICIENCY as she stood from her desk and snatched up the reports she had to give to her boss. As chilled and stiff as she'd been all week.

She pushed open the door to his office with no hesitation, her heels echoing through the blankness within.

He, as usual, didn't look up from his computer. His arm lay casually across the desk as he scrolled down the screen.

"The projections you wanted from Luke. Sir." The folder hit his desk not half as hard as she would have liked, only an inch from his hand.

He might have flinched when she said *Sir* in a near sneer. Might have, but she couldn't be entirely sure. Maybe she just wished he had.

"Thank you," he said to his screen. He was still as polite as ever—*please, thank you, could you*—but there was a hollowness there, as if he were only going through the motions.

Well, so was she.

He never met her eyes anymore. He gave her no lingering glances, no half smiles when he caught her looking. She hadn't realized how much he'd done those things until he suddenly didn't.

She was glad he didn't. Meeting the implacability in his gaze, seeing the evidence of his resolve, his need to push her away—it might break her.

Three more months. At least he wasn't going to refuse to accept her resignation now.

"Get Ronald on the phone."

"Of course." As smoothly emotionless as he had been. "Once I do that, I'll be leaving to meet with the sheriff."

She didn't imagine the flinch this time. All of him went to iron, the pretense of ignoring her lost in that moment.

"You don't need my permission," he said, low and stark.

"Oh, I wasn't asking for it," she said, wanting to hurt him with her insouciance. "I was just telling you where I'd be."

His fingers curled into a fist, and he drew his hand back as if he couldn't bear to even be that close to her.

Which was fine. She couldn't bear to be this close to him either.

"I'll get your call started." She went for the door, keeping all of her attention on leaving and not on him behind her. Her fingers curled around the knob—

"Pilar."

Had he really said her name? It was barely a whisper if he had—too soft to tell if there was any yearning within it.

She was imagining the yearning. Completely imagining it. And maybe even imagining that he'd spoken her name.

Keeping her hand tight on the doorknob, she turned to look back at him.

He wasn't watching her. He was studying the report she'd tossed on his desk, as if she weren't even there. As if she'd never been there.

He hadn't called her name. He wasn't even thinking of her.

She turned and wrenched the door open. Fine. She wouldn't think of him either. Besides, she had more important things to fret over.

When she arrived at the sheriff's office twenty minutes later, Javier was waiting for her, thank God. He'd been coming home every night this week, eating dinner with her and conversing like a normal person instead of a surly Neanderthal. They talked mostly about inconsequential stuff—nothing at all about Javier's job or his future and nothing about Benedict and her future.

Once they figured out what was happening with these charges, they could discuss what was next.

She smiled at her brother, trying to keep her relief out of the expression. He'd get pissed if she let on that she'd thought he might not show up. He was dressed for work, in heavy navy-blue pants, thick-soled boots, and a shirt with his name stitched across it.

She had to admit he looked good. He looked happy. Even if it wasn't the work outfit she would have chosen for him.

"Ready?" she asked.

"Yep." No sullenness, no sniping.

She'd have to remember to take that image out later and savor it. "Let's go."

The sheriff was kindly in that distant way many authority figures had. He wasn't against them, but he wasn't yet for them either. She could work with that.

"Thank you for meeting with us," she began after shaking his hand. He'd been the one to request the meeting, which she'd thought a bit odd—did the sheriff himself handle these things?—but she knew better than to question it. He'd wanted to meet, so here they were.

"No problem. And how are you, young man?" he asked Javier.

"Fine. Sir."

Perfect. Javier was playing the upstanding young man. That would help.

"Good, good." The sheriff folded his hands across his belly, his mouth pursing. "I have to tell you, the store wanted to press charges."

She released a slow breath. Okay. That wasn't good, but there were ways around that. "Your officers searched Javier and didn't find any stolen items." That had to count for something, didn't it?

"I know," he said. "But the manager claims that the security footage shows a man fitting your brother's description committing the other thefts."

She wondered how to tackle that. Hispanic male, late teens, early twenties—wasn't that always the suspect in these kinds of things? But she couldn't say that outright.

"Oh," she said lamely. Maybe they could get a copy of the security footage.

And then what? Convince the manager it wasn't Javier?

"Now, I talked with the manager—after I talked to Benedict Merrill," the sheriff went on.

"Benedict? You talked to Benedict?" Shit. What had he said? No doubt he'd suggested that the sheriff lock up Javier and throw away the key.

She'd kill him. No matter that he was her boss. No matter that she might be in love with him.

The sheriff looked at her oddly. "Well, yes. I understood that Mr. Merrill spoke with your brother as well."

She turned the stink eye on Javier, who simply looked away.

"Anyway," the sheriff said, "I talked to the manager and explained that Javier has no record and has never been accused of anything like this before. That he's about to graduate high school, he already has a job, and he'd be entering vocational school in the fall."

She dumbly absorbed that recitation. How did this sheriff know all this? How did *he* know and *she* didn't?

Vocational school. In the fall. When had that happened?

"Considering too that there was no real evidence your brother had done it," the sheriff continued, oblivious to her confusion, "I convinced the manager to drop the charges."

She blinked. It was over then. Javier was rescued.

But not by her. *Talked to Benedict*, indeed. Benedict had engineered this somehow. She could tell.

His frigid act all week, his insistence that she let Javier take his punishment—and all along he'd been arranging this. Behind her back.

Oh yes, she was definitely going to kill him, once she thanked him for getting her brother off.

"That's great to hear," she said with forced cheer. "I can't thank you enough."

"When Benedict and I discussed it, we agreed that this young man has a bright future."

She ground her teeth together at the mention of that name.

"We wouldn't want something like this to mar it," the sheriff finished.

"No," she got out through a tight jaw. "We certainly wouldn't. Thank you very much."

And outside again, to have yet another confrontation in front of the sheriff's station.

The sun was dipping low, the afternoon light fading into evening. It should have all been so perfect: a beautiful night, her brother out of legal trouble and off to some kind of school.

But she felt like tearing a phone book apart with her bare hands. Javier bounded out with a wide smile, which she most certainly didn't return.

"What's the matter?" he said, his face falling. "Aren't you happy?"

She stared at him for long moments, in that uniform that looked too old for him. He looked too adult, too responsible. What would their parents say if they could see him in that uniform?

She couldn't say. They were gone and it was just her and Javier. She supposed it only mattered what they said to each other—not what their parents might have said.

"I am happy," she said slowly. "And a little confused. And... hurt."

He ducked his head. "I guess I should have told you I talked to Benedict. But he asked me not to." He dug the toe of his heavy boot into the sidewalk, like he'd used to do with his sneakers when he was little. "Benedict's a good guy. He likes you."

Benedict was *not* a good guy. Good was uncomplicated. Easy. Good didn't go behind her back.

Liked her. She wasn't even touching that one.

"When did you talk to Benedict?" she asked quietly.

"He called me the day after the... arrest. Said he was sorry for thinking I was guilty when there was no proof."

He might have said so to her as well. The jerk.

Javier went on. "Benedict had Ángel come talk to the sheriff and explain about my job. And, uh, he helped with the vocational school stuff."

That familiar irritation rose in her. She'd saved so much for him to go to college. Vocational school seemed like a waste.

Benedict knew how desperately she wanted Javier to go to college, and he was helping her brother go to vocational school? How could he do that?

She was going to stop this nonsense right now.

Pilar, you be ready to listen. Really listen.

Pilar had promised Ms. Ramirez she'd do just that—if Javier would talk to her.

Javier was finally talking to her about the future.

She had to listen, no matter how hard it was.

"Tell me about the vocational school," she said, trying to be upbeat.

"It's great. Benedict took me to see it. They have this amazing CNC machine. You should see the stuff the students have made on it." His hands flew wide, his eyes sparkling, all of him animated with his excitement.

"A CNC machine, huh?" She didn't know what that was, but it seemed to make Javier happy.

"Yeah, and they have all kinds of awesome classes. I've already found like twenty I want to take."

Her own mood lightened as Javier went on. He was so excited and happy and exactly how she'd hoped he'd be about college.

"It's in the valley," Javier was saying. "So not far away at all." He looked hopefully at her. "You can visit really easily."

Only if she stayed in Cabrillo—which she wasn't.

Was she?

"Yeah," she said finally. "I can."

But it wasn't convincing enough, because Javier's face fell again. "Look, I know you really, really wanted me to go to college. And I know you saved all that money. But... but that's not what I want."

"Why didn't you tell me you wanted to go there instead of college?" She might not have worried so much if she'd known he had a plan.

"I tried, but you never listened."

He was right. She never had listened to him, had only tried to push and prod him into something he didn't want to do.

"I'm listening now," she promised. "And if this is really what you want to do—if you'll give it your all—I'll support you."

"Does that mean... will I be able to use that money for vocational school? I mean, I know it's yours and you wanted me to use it for college, and now that you're going back to school you can use it—"

She punched him gently in the shoulder, wanting to hug him but knowing it would be a bad idea in front of the sheriff's office. "Yes, you can use the money. I was saving it for you, not myself."

His expression went solemn. "I'm really sorry things between us have been bad lately. It's just—you gave up everything to raise me, and I knew you had to resent it. And then you kept saying things about what Mom and Dad would have wanted, but they're gone, and we'd never really know..." He took a deep breath. "It made me mad."

Good Lord. She'd wanted him to talk to her, but this was like a dam breaking. "Wow. Has anyone ever told you that you talk a lot?"

He laughed. "Sorry. I had to let it out."

"I'm glad you did." She set her hand on his shoulder, as close as she dared come to giving him a hug. "And I never resented taking care of you. It was my privilege. And my pleasure. You're my brother. I'll always love you. And I love the time we spend together. Even when you're being a little shit."

He ducked his head as he laughed. This felt so good, to clear the air between them. To laugh with each other again.

Why hadn't she listened to him sooner?

"I should tell you," Javier said, "I was pissed at Benedict too. I should have been taking care of the tires and the sink. But I let it slide 'cause I was pissed about the college stuff. And then he took care of it all and I was mad at him. And myself. But it's okay now. We made up. So you two can be together."

Her mouth dropped open. Did he really think it would be that simple? Javier gave his blessing and *boom*—she and Benedict lived happily ever after.

"No," she said with deliberation. "Things are okay between you and me—we just need to remember that you have to talk and I have to listen—but things are most certainly not okay between Benedict and me. Things are pretty fucking far from okay."

Javier watched her warily. "Are you... are you really that mad at him?

"Mad?" That word didn't even come close. "I'm furious. Doing all this behind my back, treating me like I was made of ice all week... Oh, yeah, he's going to get it."

She could almost taste her righteous anger—how delicious it was going to be to tell Mr. High and Mighty Benedict Merrill where he could shove it.

"Do you think he'll fire you?" Javier asked with something close to fear.

"Fire me?" she scoffed. "I've already resigned."

But she wasn't half so brave as she was pretending. She realized suddenly that it was one thing to *plan* to blast him with the flames of her anger, but actually doing it would be quite another.

And she did need this job for the next three months.

But Benedict did deserve to be chewed out.

Decisions, decisions.

"What are you going to do now?" Javier asked.

That was the million-dollar question. She clenched her jaw and set her fists on her hips. "Benedict Merrill and I are going to have it out."

Javier gave a low whistle. "Thank God I'm not him."

"When I'm finished with him," she said grimly, "he'll wish he wasn't him either."

Chapter 11

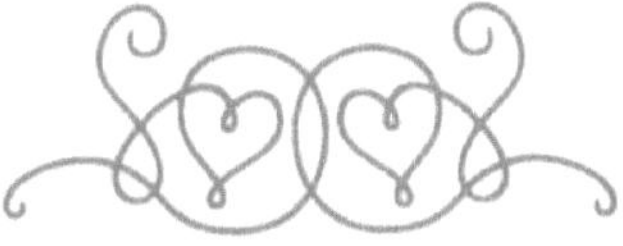

IT WAS LATE WHEN PILAR walked back into Benedict's office, but he was right where she'd left him: slumped in his chair, staring at his computer screen. She had the impression he wasn't actually seeing anything in front of him.

He glanced up when she entered, looked at her for the first time in a week, and that blue gaze hit her right in her gut. It was so sad and pleading and...

No. Be strong.

"You could have told me." No sense beating around the bush. He'd know what she meant.

"I didn't think you wanted to talk to me." Quiet yet firm.

"I didn't. But you still could have said something. And going behind my back—"

He held up a hand. "I'm going to let you give me hell since I deserve it. But I need to tell you something. Can I talk first?"

"Fine." Although she folded her arms across her chest to let him know how not into this she was. She wanted to get to the *giving him hell* part and skip all the rest.

He came around the desk, propped his hip against it, only inches from her.

An electrical fire started under her skin, smoking just out of sight. *Keep it together.* All she had to do was to listen to whatever he had to say, tell him off, then head home.

Scratching her itch for Benedict was no longer an action item.

"I talked with Josh earlier this week."

That wasn't at all what she'd been expecting. She splayed her hand on the desk, searching for balance. "You did?"

He nodded, the set of his mouth turning grim. "I didn't like it, but I did it. I told him that when he came home it would be with a blank slate."

She curled her hand into a fist to keep that mutinous appendage from reaching for him. So what if he'd apologized to his own brother? He still needed to apologize to *her*.

"Josh will have to work for my good opinion," Benedict went on. "I don't give that out for free. But I told him if he wanted a job in the stockyard and to stay in the main house, I wouldn't stop him."

"So you admitted you were wrong?" Perhaps he was ready to admit he'd been wrong about some other things too.

Maybe she wouldn't have to give him hell. Maybe she could give him a little heck instead.

"It's not my favorite thing to do," he admitted with a wry twist of his lips. "But I did it. And we... we actually talked then, Josh and I. Which we haven't done in probably ten years. Well, he talked. I listened."

She rubbed at the tears starting in her eyes. Stupid emotions, giving in to him like that. "I just did the same thing with Javier."

"How did it go?" So gentle, his voice. She wanted to just fall into his arms.

No. No, she didn't. She was still mad at him. Even though she was crying at what he'd said.

"Fine," she said. "Thanks for talking with the sheriff and getting Javier into that vocational school." She took a deep breath and squared her shoulders. "And I'm also really fucking pissed about it. And that you acted like you were mad at me all week."

Oh, that had hurt to get out—she was feeling very shaky as well as weepy. But it had to be said.

He rubbed his neck. "If you want... if you're that angry"—pain flared in his eyes—"you can quit now. I'll pay the three months salary, as severance."

Charity. More charity. "You just can't help it can you?" she burst out. "I've been your charity case my entire life and you *just can't stop.*"

His face went bone white and he looked as ill as she felt. "I—no, I can't help it. When I care about someone, I want to protect them. I want to protect you."

She closed her eyes, his expression too painful to bear. "I'm still leaving," she said. "There is nothing you could say that would convince me to stay. Nothing."

"I know." A raw whisper. "Even if there were, I wouldn't say it. Because you deserve this opportunity to have something for yourself."

Benedict suffers in silence. She opened her eyes, his beloved face once more in her sight. Her gut knotted. "Were you ever going to tell me what you did for Javier?"

"I didn't mean to keep it a secret forever. I wanted to fix everything for you so you wouldn't have to worry about it. I was so damn sick of you worrying about everything. And I wasn't mad. It just... it hurt to be near you all day, but not with you."

She released a small, sobbing breath. "It hurt me too. And those things you said about my brother..." She bit her lip. She had to get ahold of herself. The tears were small at the moment—she couldn't let them get any bigger. Couldn't let this confrontation break her down.

He did the eyebrow thing. "You said some pretty harsh stuff about my brother yourself. But you were right—Javier isn't Josh. You once asked me what I would have done differently with my brother. I said nothing, but I was wrong. If I had known from the beginning where Josh would end up, I wouldn't have let Dad hush up his first DUI. I would have made Josh take the full punishment."

She sniffled long and loud, because she couldn't hold out much longer, not when he was admitting so beautifully that he'd been wrong. He caught up her hand, and she let him, because it felt so good.

She wiped her eyes with her free hand. Damn it, she didn't want to cry. Her fingertips came away smeared with mascara. Great. Now she probably looked like a depressed raccoon.

"I planned all this stuff for Javier," she got out. "And he... he wants something so different. Was I wrong to want college for him so badly?"

"No. But he's got his own path to walk. Just like Josh will when he gets out. Doesn't mean that you and I won't worry about them or wonder how things could have been different." His face took on a considering frown. "Speaking of Javier, do you know how much Ángel's shop clears in profit each year?"

She shrugged. "No. He must have a large overhead, buying parts and paying labor though."

Benedict smiled. "That's a very accountant like answer. Yes, he does have high costs. But he makes five million a year. After taxes."

Five million? "What? How do you know that?"

His shoulders slumped sheepishly. "I, uh, gave him some start up funds a while back."

"Of course you did." How like Benedict. "And I'm still going to worry about Javier, even if he is getting into a multi-million dollar business." She laughed, although it only held a touch of humor. "We're a pair, aren't we?"

He went very, very still, his hand tightening on hers. Uncertainty pulled his mouth flat, made the blue of his eyes dim. "About that pair business... do you think you can help me with my worries about Josh? And I'll help you worry about Javier?"

Was he asking her to stay? Or something else? She'd been mad when she'd come flying in here on wings of indignation. But now the anger was gone and she was unsure. She'd had a plan, but did she even want that plan anymore? Did she want *him* more?

She did want to leave. But she didn't want to leave him.

"Maybe," she hedged. "You could have said something last week, instead of letting us both stew."

"I am the strong, silent type."

She laughed. "Yeah, you definitely are."

He was watching her so steadily. She felt like she could cling to that gaze through anything. And she wanted to. Wanted to hold tight to him.

Plans changed. And sometimes they changed for the best.

Benedict made her feel her best. When she was with him, she didn't have to be alone, trying her hardest to keep everything together. Maybe accepting his help in keeping everything together wasn't such a bad thing.

"If we're going to make this work, you're going to have to drop that act around me."

His smile was bright enough to melt an ice cap. "You want to make this work?"

She did. She really did. She could go out and find more in that wide, wide world, but such discoveries were only worth it if she had Benedict to come home to.

She nodded, and he tugged her into his arms where she nuzzled her face into his shirtfront. He smelled so good.

"Yes," she said.

And that was that. Staying, going—she wasn't certain how they'd work that out, but they'd manage. They were smart.

He took a deep breath. "I won't ask you to stay here in Cabrillo. We can do a long-distance thing, a casual thing, whatever you want."

But his arms around her grew tense, and she knew that while he might say such things, he didn't want to let her go. But at least he was offering.

"And I have to warn you—I'm going to want to fix things for you. Your car, your sink, your brother's legal troubles. I can't help it. I know that bugs you sometimes, but... but I love doing things for you. Making your life easier."

Love. He said he loved every inch of her, loved doing things for her...

Benedict's crazy about you.

She wrapped her arms around his waist, grabbed two fistfuls of shirt, and looked up at him. Willing him to say what she wanted to hear.

"About dropping the strong, silent bit around you...," he

began. His swallow was loud in the silence. "I'm in love with you. I have been for years."

"For *years*? But you never... Not even once."

He loved her. He had for years. She was going to need a moment to process that.

Talk about going behind her back...

"When did this happen?" Because she'd never guessed, not once.

"Oh, it probably started when you walked into my office that first time, holding your resume, looking so brave." His smile was so warm, so... *loving*, her heart squeezed.

She blinked hard. "You never said anything. Never even hinted." Her voice was thick with all she was holding in.

"You were raising Javier," he said, "and I didn't want to complicate your life. Once he graduated, I planned to make my move."

Okay, maybe she was going to need more than a moment to process it. Because she was still muddled. *He loved her.*

And she loved him? Right?

"And when I announced I was leaving?" she asked, stalling for some time to think.

"Yeah." His grin was so adorable. "I had to accelerate things then."

It was the grin that did it. That and the fact he'd admitted he was wrong, even though he'd hated it.

She *did* love him. Loved his resolve, his concern for his family, the way he gave back to their community... and she loved the way he cared for her. Even when he was being all strong and silent about it.

Really, would she have been tempted to change her plans for anything less than love?

Because she loved him, knew that he loved her, she said

next: "I'm still leaving. I want to finish my certification. I need that for myself."

"If you need it, I want you to have it."

The tears almost started up again.

"We might not see each other very often," she said.

"I can visit each weekend."

"And if I'm really far away?"

"We do have a private jet."

Of course they did. "What about your carbon footprint?" She grinned at him.

He laughed, then sobered. "Do you think you could come back someday?"

He couldn't leave Cabrillo. She knew better than to ask that. But he wouldn't demand that she stayed. He wanted her to make the choice.

He didn't know that she already had.

"Yeah, I'll be coming back. Because, you see, I'm in love with you too."

He'd looked like that before, as if he'd just been granted his heart's desire, when he'd first seen her undressed. But this time it was lighter, brighter, more open. Almost painful in its intensity.

He planted a kiss on the corner of her mouth, and it felt so right to have him do it. Then his mouth claimed hers, and she forgot about everything as she kissed him back.

Man, she was going to get to do this all the time now. And in public.

Well, maybe not in public, because they were going to be tearing off clothes in a second.

After a time, they pulled apart. "I don't think that was very businesslike," she panted.

"Fuck businesslike," he growled. "Although you're probably right. I should just take you home to bed."

She set a hand in the middle of his chest. "Can't. I have to go home to feed Javier."

He groaned. "Can I invite myself to dinner at least?"

"Of course, but keep your hands to yourself. We don't want to corrupt my little brother."

He snorted at that, but she could tell he was amused. God, but she loved to tickle his sense of humor.

"Only three more months, huh?" he asked.

"Yep. But don't think you'll have me at your beck and call after. I'll be very busy with school work," she reminded him primly.

"But after, you're coming back as a brand-new accountant. Which is good, because we can always use accountants. And I bet your employer will be real understanding when you need to go part-time once you start having babies." His smile tipped into a smirk, all self-satisfied male.

"Babies?" She raised an eyebrow. "Before you've asked me to marry you?"

He groaned. "Jumped the gun on that."

She patted his chest. "No, I like your plan. I finish my certification, come back to Cabrillo, we get married, and then work on some kids a few years later. One problem though—I don't know that my employer is going to be as forgiving as you assume."

He frowned. Well, he'd better get used to her not falling in line with all of his plans.

"Because I'll be working at the casino," she explained. "They need plenty of accountants there too. I wouldn't want to tempt you into harassing an employee, even if she is your wife."

She could be with him, yet still have her own career. Her own accomplishments. She wasn't his charity case.

"Fine," he grumbled. "You're right, so I won't argue."

"Ha. I'm going to file that one away since I don't think I'll be hearing it often."

He pinched her butt. "Quit giving me sass. And what's for dinner?"

"I *know* I'll be hearing that one a lot."

He grinned like a schoolboy, all happy mischief. "I'll do all the cooking if you ask me to." He sobered, went solemn. "I'll do anything you ask me to."

She kissed him, soft and sweet. "Just love me."

"I already do."

Epilogue

PILAR TAPPED OUT AN E-MAIL, hit Send, and looked around her desk. Two more months and this wouldn't be hers anymore, since she'd be off to San Diego.

Her in San Diego and Javier starting school soon—the Lopez family was doing pretty all right these days. Javier had even convinced her to drive him down to the valley so he could buy some books for school—a full two months early.

So maybe the vocational school thing was going to work out after all.

She glanced at her replacement sitting at the next desk over, a rather frightened-looking twentysomething kid named Jason. Fresh out of college, still wide-eyed and innocent.

"Did you finish the TPS reports?" she asked.

"Yeah." He fiddled with a pen. "Do you need to check them?"

She gave him a look. "*Do* I need to check them?"

"No?" He blinked. "No." Firmer. "I went through the checklist. They're correct."

"Good." He'd settle down in a bit she could tell, but until then, Benedict was going to have a time with him. She only hoped her soon-to-be-former boss didn't scare the poor kid away in the meantime.

Benedict came out of his office just then, looking like six feet of sexy cowboy deliciousness. God, she'd miss him during the week. Thank goodness she'd be having fun finishing her certification.

And he'd already promised to visit every weekend. Then they'd be having fun together. And be away from the knowing looks of his family. His siblings were more than happy for them, but Liliana just couldn't stop laughing knowingly every time she saw them together. Pilar could understand now why Benedict told his sister to get lost whenever she came upon him and Pilar together.

"Ready for lunch?" he asked. What he meant was *Ready to get off company property so we can make out in my truck?*

Yes. Yes, she was.

She grabbed her purse. "You'll be okay, Jason?"

"Yeah," he said unsteadily. "Any calls, I forward them to you, right?"

"Nope. You can handle it." She patted his shoulder when he went pale. "You're ready." She turned to Benedict. "Let's go."

When they hit the hallway—and were out of Jason's sight—Benedict grabbed her and kissed her. "Been waiting to do that all day," he grumbled.

"No, you haven't," she reminded him. "Have you already forgotten this morning? And now I have to go fix my lipstick."

"I'm just gonna mess it up again."

"I know, but I want to walk out of here not looking like I'm doing a walk of shame. Give me a second."

They really needed to invent a Benedict-proof lip stain, she thought as she walked toward the bathroom. She was running through her stockpile way too fast.

Maybe she should have him buy stock in the cosmetics company—not that he needed any more money.

When she walked into the bathroom, she found Liliana staring into the mirror above the sink. Tears were rolling down her cheeks.

"Oh sweetie, what's wrong?" She pulled Liliana in for a hug, patting at her shoulder. Pilar had never seen Benedict's sister even close to crying.

"Everything," the other woman wailed.

Oh dear. It wasn't at all like Liliana to say something like that. Pilar patted her shoulder some more. "What's wrong? Is there anything I can do?"

"Yes." Liliana sniffled and squared her shoulders. "You can help me figure out how to tell Benedict that I'm pregnant."

WANT MORE HOT COWBOY ROMANCE? Pick up *Her Bull Rider's Baby,* the next in A Cowboy of Her Own! Keep reading for a sneak peek!

About the Author

Genevieve Turner is a *USA Today* bestselling author of western romance. She loves cowboys, the rural life, and happily ever afters. She lives in beautiful Southern California with the perfect number of kids, dogs, and turkeys—and probably too many chickens.

You can find her on the web at www.genturner.com.

Genevieve's Newsletter

NEW RELEASES, SALES, AND A *Free* STARTER LIBRARY WHEN YOU SIGN UP!

CLICK HERE